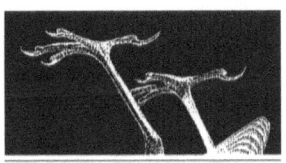

I0673332

Publication Studio | EBM Edition

Virility Rituals of

North American Teenage Boys

stories

Matt Briggs

for Lisa

The author would like to thank the editors of magazines where
stories in this collection previously appeared: *Birkensnake, The
Chicago Review, Filter Magazine, MonkeyBicycle, Roethke
Readings, Spork,* and *TRNSF Magazine.*

Proofread by Michael Peck

Publication Studio
publicationstudio.biz

This is a work of fiction and everything contained herein is
fabricated, even the names of people, places, and things that
have some resemblance to those in the real world.

Virility Rituals of North American Teenage Boys

Contents

The League of Bears

My wife bloomed in her late thirties. She had always been pretty, but pretty in a cute kind of way. Her inner geek trumped any fashion sense. When our old Mac PowerBook, which was known for running way too hot—hot enough to leave second degree burns—cooked its hard drive, she was the one who unscrewed the lid and cut open the protective foil with an X-Acto knife to swap the drive. Late in the summer of her 37th year, she experienced a transformation. She lost a bit of weight. She focused her geeky energy on vintage dresses. She began a regime of mild exercise and became sexy, as if it were a hobby.

I, on the other hand, began my rapid decline into middle age. I had expected this based on the physical appearance of my uncles. They were short, bald, fat hermits who lived frustrated lives of randy irritability.

If you subscribe to *The Theory of Leagues*, as in "she is in his league" or "she is out of his league," my wife had been drafted by the majors. By comparison, I was about to be dropped from the community pick-up game. She had become beautiful. I had become grotesque.

During this time, my contract ended at an online travel company. I found work at a government agency that was willing to pay me a ridiculous sum of money to sit at a desk and read articles I'd pasted from the Web into MS Word. I wasn't allowed to surf. Occasionally the manager who'd hired me would call me into her office to yell. Not fluent in the acronyms of the agency, I had no idea what she was talking about. Shaken, I would return to my desk and continue my gradual decline.

The only person who would talk to me was another large man with a hairless scalp compensated for by a very thick beard. He was named Chuck. Except for his luxuriant beard and biker-fashion sense, Chuck was my spitting image. He was big. He said, "Hope you hang in there, buddy."

The fact of my wife's massively increased sexiness became a problem. At no point did my wife appear aware of the gap between us. It seemed obvious that if we had been in a crowd of refugees, I would have been sorted into the cattle cars carrying the brutish people off to do field work. She would have a plush seat on the air-conditioned tour bus whisking her to her desk job, where they had complimentary bottles of iced seltzer.

The gap permeated everything. I have never been self-conscious about—how do I say this—*autoerotic stimulation.* I could only limit my fantasy life to the plausible. I became a devotee of homely porn.

Searching online for homely porn is harder than you would think. Given enough people with enough privacy just about anything you could imagine, or would care not to imagine, is found erotic by some group of people somewhere. In my Google survey for homely porn I ran the risk of seeing things that I didn't want to see. I discovered, for instance, a number of men who like to wear diapers and stuff them with simulated mess. They posted recipes of the mess formula depending on their poo preference: light, dark, creamy, chunky. I discovered a community with a predilection for images of people having sex dressed up as kittens, robots, aliens. People liked to have sex in gobs of food or dayglo. I discovered a site with page after page of pictures of men like me who apparently were the erotic fixation of men who liked big men. They called them bears. There didn't seem to be a female interest in bears. I discovered that for just about anyone, even adults who wore diapers or dressed in latex kitten outfits, everyone belonged to a league of some kind.

When I hear the phrase *a sexless marriage*, I can't help but think there is some underlying dysfunction. An essential part of a couple is broken or decoupled. I wanted my own bed. I wanted a gap of space between my heaving, snoring mass, and my wife's pretty floral PJs and her mass of curly hair. I wanted something Ozzie and Harriet-style. "Don't you want to sleep with me?" my wife asked. "In the same bed?" I could not explain. I was worried I would roll over in the middle of the night and wake to find her plastered to the side of my mole-covered back like a tattoo.

Normally, I ate huge amounts of food. If I didn't eat a meal every three hours, I would get light-headed. I didn't snack, but I ate regularly. Now I only ate egg whites for breakfast and a sliver of chicken breast for dinner. I walked around frustrated by my inability with my wife and now famished. I began to go running. One day at work, I told Chuck that I was thinking about going running at lunch. I asked about good places to jog. He told me about the private showers for employees.

"Are you getting in even better shape?"

"I need to lose a few pounds," I said.

"How many?"

"About two hundred and thirty," I said. "Something like that."

"Hell no you don't," he said. "Some people like their boys big."

"I suppose," I said.

"I'll be angry with you if you destroy what you have."

"I have a lot of what I have, Chuck," I said.

He shook his head. "Diets don't work," he said. "You got to make do with the lot you've drawn in life." In theory, I agreed with this. Actually, though, I expected things to get better every year, for my life to gradually improve until I eventually died in a fit of hysterical joy. Settling, by comparison, seemed boring.

My wife and I tried to overcome my problem. I could not ask for a more patient problem solver. The final session before I admitted to myself that something was irreparable, she said, "Why don't you look at some porn while we do it?" She got the old Apple Powerbook and found some filthy video on YouPorn, "the YouTube of porn." I found a grandmother type who was actually quite old. She had thick moles on her face with gray squiggly hairs coming out and lines around the edge of her mouth. There was a grayish stain on her brown dress left by the fragment of a muffin. There was a plumber who apparently did his plumbing naked except for his Oshkosh overalls. For homely porn, it was very promising.

I didn't know where to put the laptop. While we were going at it, we tried to place it on the nightstand. I couldn't see anything. Finally, I placed it on my wife's stomach. As a laptop with legs, she was kind of like a porno-Teletubby. However, the homely clip was only a minute and a half-long. The clip ended. I fiddled with the track pad. My fingers were slick from sweat; the pad hardly responded to the tip of my fingers. I managed to get the clip to play again. Over and over again this happened until my wife started to sob. "I can't take it anymore!" The Powerbook's overheated case burned her stomach. She hopped out of bed. She ran into the bathroom to spray the red blotch on her stomach with cold water. We slept that night in our bed as if we were sleeping in two separate beds.

I didn't know who to talk to. I suppose there are sex therapists. There are pills. I could see a mesmerist. At work, I mentioned to Chuck that this friend of my mine had this problem. Chuck said, well, he knew how he could help this guy out. "A guy like that just needs to know some people find him irresistible."

"How?" I asked. I imagined he knew some doctor who might have the right kind of tincture or pharmaceutical.

"He won't be sorry," he said. "He has a clinical problem. No one would blame him for getting help."

I wasn't sure what kind of help Chuck had in mind. I was desperate to close this gap that had appeared between me and my wife, between me and all other human beings on the planet. I made the necessary arrangements and then after work I went to the address Chuck had recommended to my friend. It was a condo, a nice one. The grounds were immaculate. There was a wind chime outside that played actual, in tune music as the wind blew. Wait a minute, I thought, this isn't a clinic. I went in anyway.

Chuck opened the door. "Hi," I said. He was not in the least surprised to see me. His condo was fastidiously clean. He had flowers on a vase on the deck. He had Spanish beer in the fridge. Chuck was the only one there.

"We've talked about my wife," I said. "I am married to a remarkably attractive woman."

"Well good for you," he said. "But sometimes the remarkably attractive is not what you need."

"I'm a straight man," I said.

"Do they issue straight people paperwork now?" Chuck said.

"My license just has my eye color and weight," I said.

"Is your weight really accurate on your license?" Chuck asked.

I shrugged. Later, as Chuck had me in a leather truss hanging over his beautifully appointed bed and brushed his massive beard on my massive stomach, and everything felt, well, massive. To have my desire make me an object of desire was good. I found myself doing something unfair to Chuck. I had my eyes closed, and found myself imaging I was a woman instead. The woman was my wife.

Virility Rituals of North American Teenage Boys

An Uncontrolled Swelling

My cousin's nuts started to swell after we returned from a late summer camping trip with my father. We had slept in a tent in the mountains and my cousin, Frankie, had left his underwear outside overnight and I told him not to put them back on. He had no idea what kind of bug could get into his shorts overnight, but like a doofus he had only packed one pair of underwear, so he slept in his swimming trunks during the night and then, in the morning, he put on his underpants by the hot air of the camp fire. A pair of underpants, grayish and stained in the heavily used regions between the legs, was not something we wanted to see while eating our morning oatmeal. "We don't want to have to look at your stinky briefs," my father said, so Frankie put them back on. "They're making my nuts cold," he said. We broke down camp and began to hike further into the mountains, around this big lake, and finally, at the end of the day, we were way into the backcountry. Aside from the trail, the only sign that there were people on the earth were the scratches of contrails in the sky, and of course the three of us.

Frankie started itching at the lake and, by the time we got to the camp, he couldn't wear his briefs anymore. My father gave him some lotion and that helped a little. He just wore his shorts, and Frankie said it didn't itch anymore. But from his frequent trips behind the bushes, I could tell he was still scratching. At that camp, my dad and I went fishing and Frankie just hung out at the camp, doing his homework. He had brought his homework out into the forest with us. I don't know what that was about. When we got back, we didn't think about it anymore. Every now and then I noticed he was scratching down there, and I didn't say anything. If he needed to scratch, then scratch, that's how I thought about it. We got back to the car and drove home, and he was still scratching. I said something then because it is one thing to be all scratchy out in the wilderness and another thing to be scratchy in public. And the car was practically public.

"Man," I said. "Why are you scratching?"

"Because it itches," he said.

He jumped out of the car, and it started then. The swelling.

He couldn't go to school the next week because something had happened to his ball sack. It had started to grow, and by Monday morning was the size of a softball. By the end of the week, it was like a volleyball.

His mother took him to the doctor.

The doctor said his balls were full of fluid. They tried to drain his balls with a needle. They stuck it right in. Frankie said they sprayed his nuts with something to numb them, but it still must have hurt. When I asked him, Frankie just said, "Well—" and made a face.

After that first visit, they grew to the size of a medicine ball.

The whole family was over at Frankie's house, and we couldn't say, like, what's wrong with him? We were all worried about Frankie, but we also made sure to wash our hands a whole lot because no one wanted to get what he had. I for one didn't use the bathroom in his house. He sat in his room, and he was fine except for this blanket that lay over him and this shape between his legs. That shape was his ball sack. "So what's wrong?" I asked him from the door. "Did they get inflamed from scratching?"

"Leave me alone," Frankie said.

"Does it hurt?"

"No. It doesn't hurt, but it still itches, and I can't scratch it. Mom says if I do, they might pop."

"So what is it?"

"Elephantiasis," he said.

"What?"

"Elephantitis of the nuts. But it's really just Elephantiasis."

I didn't have anything to say to that. I felt bad for him. I'd been out in those woods, too. It could have been me, just as much as him.

That weekend it got bad. He called me and said that he thought he might die. They said it was infected, too, and that if it burst, "I'll bleed to death in seconds." He said, "I'll bleed to death from burst balls." Frankie started to cry. He had called me because I'd been there the whole time. Because it could have been me as much as him.

I said, "Hang in there, Frankie. The doctors know what they are doing."

They had given him some medication and drained his ball sack and then gradually the swelling went down, and then finally we were all at Frankie's house and he was walking around in a pair of jeans and seemed just fine. He shook his head. "I can't go back to school, you know," he said.

"They'll get over it," I said. "They'll just be jealous because their balls are all normal sized."

He didn't go back though. He enrolled at the community college and finished that way. He just didn't go back to school. Once your balls get the size of your head, I suppose that makes you an adult.

Erection

My penis began its testing sequence in the middle of seventh grade. In language arts, Mrs. Gilgi lectured on the expository essay. We had read Mark Twain, E.B. White, and some dry, succinct passages written for the seventh grade reading level—passages I found almost incomprehensible. It was late November. It was early morning and foggy outside. The maple trees that grew at the age of the athletic field lay like black streaks against pale, illuminated walls. Dew covered the blades of grass that had grown too long in the drizzle, because the groundskeepers were waiting for a cold snap to leave things dry enough to mow. The radiator ticked and fizzled, emitting a rusty heat. There was nothing in the room remotely arousing at 8:23 a.m. Gilgi had long hair that didn't hang down her head but rather curled and frayed in a thicket over her head. She wore long turquoise earrings, a sack-like dress, and wool socks secured with the rawhide straps of Birkenstocks. She was as sexless as EB White. The lights in the room: florescent tubes with a sanitized, unrelenting glare enhanced by the buffed and pocked linoleum flooring. And yet, in this room, my penis began a testing sequence. I was at my desk. I shifted, and then it grew, and locked into position and began, well, began to pulse. By this, I mean the sides throbbed. The head flared and then relaxed and flared and relaxed. I almost ran out of the room, but could not move. I waited and wondered if I was having a seizure. Perhaps this was the last thing that happened to someone before they died? But, the test sequence ran its course, and I learned then that I had to be prepared for mid-region random drills. My body did not entirely belong to me anymore.

Virility

O ur bodies were inadvertently virile. I played *Dungeons & Dragons* and spent too much time trying to incorporate the Succubus into the game, based solely on the monster's cleavage and *Playboy* pose. In high school, boys had mustaches. In an era of wide tires on V8s, a time of striped shirts exposing chest hair and a single, glittering strand of gold chain, an epoch of white and tan blue jeans stretched tight across the ass and tight at the ankles, any hair on a lip was not to be scorned but cultivated. Several boys wore long, drooping Fu Manchu mustaches. One kid had a beard. But for me, as soon as hair began to show on my upper lip, I began to shave. Gradually the hair turned into thick, sharp stubble. By the last bell at 2:20, I had five o'clock shadow. I had to take driver's education to get a permit to drive. My body, however, was already moving toward something and I didn't know what it was, but I had heard rumors.

I was new to the middle school. I walked to school with the stoners who lived in the derelict ramblers near the pipeline. This area was older and developed in haphazard swathes compared to the planned unit development where I lived. My house sat behind sidewalks, and a two-lane road edged with storm drains. The gravel roads in the stoner's territory were edged with deep ditches full of cattails. The occasional drunk driver tipped into the ditch. The houses lay far back from the road, past thickets of blackberries and rusting cars. The Stoners wore black jean jackets, black Levis, and white Reebok's shredded and stained from mowing lawns over the summer. They didn't carry backpacks. Instead, they each carried a single slim folder adorned with the names of guitar bands, a notebook, a pencil stuffed into the O-wire. Jason was doing it with a neighborhood woman. "I mow her lawn, and let's say, I haven't been earning very much money," he said.

This seemed as implausible to me as it did to the rest of the stoners. He said, "You don't believe me?" We followed him down the gravel road, and waited in the fir trees under the power line, while he checked around the house. And then, he knocked on the door.

What is he doing?

The door opened, and a woman who must have been in her thirties opened it. Understand, at 15, "in her thirties" is a perfect age for a woman to be. She wore blue jeans and a sweat shirt. He leaned in to kiss her. He clasped her shoulder and pulled her toward him. And then he let his hand fall across her chest and he grabbed her breast.

"Did you see that?"

He stepped into the house without even looking back at us, and the door closed.

We said all at once: "A woman like that must know something. What does she see in him? His feet smell. I think he's been wearing the same socks for the last week. How does something like this happen?"

We didn't know.

We walked on the trail through the forest, ruminating over what this meant, but we didn't know. If our own bodies were mysterious (as they were) then a woman's body was completely unknowable. We'd studied the literature for clues, but it only provided us with an understanding of the literature. Revelations about the world where we lived remained untranslated.

Russ, Our Zombie For A Pet

L ately, we had taken to drinking too much gin at my
friend Laura's apartment. I picked Erin and Sarah
up, and we drove over to Laura's place. Laura had
enrolled in theatrical makeup class in the evening. She had
given up her aspirations as an actress, not because she
wasn't good enough, but pragmatically, she wanted to be
paid. Her boss moved her from the evening hostess staff at
the grill to the lunchtime wait staff. Laura worked fewer
hours, made more money, and began to buy really excellent
gin, Bombay Sapphire. As a group we hadn't really been
drinkers. But with this square blue bottle, drinking became
an activity. In the climate of the four of us not really
knowing anything about ourselves, a whole bunch of gin

was a relief. We really didn't know what was going on and after a few tonics didn't care.

Before Laura had enrolled in her makeup class, Laura had worn her lips as red as they would bear. We could always find her glass because it was the one with the greasy transparent pink residue. Her face was as white as a department store sink. But, given her new mastery of the art of face painting, she suddenly looked natural and freshly beautiful. There had always been some guy hanging around as her boyfriend, but they were usually the type who would come over to change the oil in her car. In her sudden transformation she started to date Russ, a pre-med, ironed-clothes wearing, well-rounded guy. He was, on the surface, a different class of guy. He couldn't change the oil in her car, but he could meet her at the library for a study date.

There was a security gate in the lobby of Laura's building. Laura had long ago given us the code. The hallway of her apartment smelled of people's amateur cooking: curry, boiling beans, seared plastic spatulas. The muffled laugh track of a sitcom pierced the walls. We knocked and could hear a growing murmur of voices in Laura's apartment. Laura flung open the door. A massive black eye lay like a saucer on her eye. The skin had started to green around the edges.

"Should we come in?" I asked. But before Laura could say anything, Erin had wedged herself in the door.

"How did you get that black eye?" Erin asked.

"What black eye?"

"Guys!" Russ called out from somewhere in the

apartment.

Erin closed the door behind Laura leaving Laura in the hallway with us. "We want a moment alone with you," Erin said.

"What's going on?" Laura asked. She was so nervous she looked as if she was about to cry or laugh. The skin trembled around the edge of her mouth.

Erin shook her head. "Come on," she said.

"Oh," Laura said. She passed her fingers over the saucer-sized purple ring. "It's nothing. I'm allergic to my makeup or something."

"Right," Erin said. She opened the door and walked down the hallway, her shoulders set. We followed. Laura closed herself in the bathroom, presumably to inspect her wound. Erin threw herself down on the couch. "So Russ. What's the story with her eye?"

Russ was in the kitchen cooking something. He had Laura's apron on, plaid with lace margins, a large monogrammed "L" on the breast pocket. "She walked into a doorknob," he said, "or whatever she said."

I didn't say anything, being conspicuously of the male gender.

When Laura returned, her black eye was gone.

"What?" Erin asked.

"Makeup," Laura said.

"That," Erin said, "was not funny."

While we drank and played poker, Laura worked on Russ' face until she'd given him a gruesome facial scar that looked like a big seam in his face. Purple lay deep in the fold. The rest of his skin looked white from supposed blood loss. He looked dead. When I said he looked like a zombie, he started to shuffle around. He began to get warm from the makeup and the gin, so he took off his clothes.

"Dude," Erin said, "put your clothes back on."

He started to put back on his pants but became confused by the number of pant legs.

He'd do anything else we asked him. He was like a puppy dog and not a full-grown man. A full-grown man would be modest about his nakedness, but Russ didn't care. I was plowed, but I wasn't about to get naked like some fool.

Erin said again, "Dude, put your clothes on."

Laura, clearly thrilled by Russ' nudity in front of us, asked me, "What do you think of him?"

"I'm not taking off my clothes," I said.

"Hey Zombie Russ," I said, "Why don't you go outside as a zombie?"

And Russ said, "All right," and then he made this zombie noise. "Must eat brains," he shouted. He opened the apartment door and left

It was pretty much the middle of the night in the neighborhood where Laura lived. Just shadowy sidewalks. The building had long stalks of bamboo that cast stark shadows over the street from the streetlights. They rustled in the sweet smelling breeze coming up from the lake. The security gate rattled nearby. Russ was walking out there naked, shuffling like a zombie, and then a tired old man walking home from his job that must have been a job as a janitor, turned the corner. He carried his own mop. He stopped, and then Russ shuffled toward him, "Must eat brains!" Russ crooned. It didn't sound like his voice at all. We were all pretty impressed.

The janitor did something that really surprised us. I would cross the street figuring the person was drunk or something, but the janitor freaked out as if Russ really were a zombie. He ran as quickly as he could back the way he came. Russ stopped then and looked up to us and started to laugh. He returned to the apartment still laughing. "Did you see him? He ran like a chicken."

And that is when we noticed that his penis was erect.

Laura put a towel over him, and he lay down. He chuckled until he fell asleep.

"Well," we said, "that was fun." Sarah and Erin and I laughed as we left.

"He's not going to last long with her," Erin said. Erin got out at Sarah's building. "Sarah'll give me a ride home."

I kept thinking that that night, I must admit with a degree of glee, "Russ isn't going to last long."

I called Laura during the week and asked her to go for coffee, but she said she couldn't because she had planned to hang out with Russ.

"What does that entail, plans to hang out with Russ?"

"You know."

"I don't know," I said. "Does it mean eating people's brains?" I asked.

"I have a zombie for a boyfriend," she said.

"What does hanging out with Russ mean?"

"You know," she said.

"I'm slow," I said. "I don't know."

"The usual," she said.

"Which is?"

"That which two consenting adults get up to when they are alone. You know, the usual."

"Or in your case a consenting adult and a helpless zombie with wood," I said. For some reason, it had never really occurred to me that Laura was actually having sex with her boyfriends. There seemed to be a chastity associated with her boys. She rarely touched them in public. She didn't flirt. I had believed she might not yet have had sex. I thought she was saving herself for the person she really loved. That maybe she knew who she really loved. That she was somehow at heart conservative in this single way and that her being conservative in this single way was something that made her kind of strange to me. And now, her telling me she had sex removed this strange aspect of her. It made her normal.

"Do you love him?" I asked.

"Christ," she said. "He's a zombie." She started to laugh. "He's a stiff."

"I have to go," I said. "I'll see you this weekend."

"Russ and I are going to Gastown in Vancouver."

"Overnight."

"Yes. Overnight. And I didn't ask my parents about it. What is with you?"

"This seems like a serious relationship."

"He's really sweet in private. I know what he's like in public. But he is completely a different person behind closed doors."

"Right," I said. "In public, he is a drooling and

shambling member of the dead. But in private, he is lively and sweet."

"He is sweet. He's our zombie for a pet."

Although I might have thought about it in the past, it had not occurred to me that I was just hanging out until Laura noticed me. And now I realized in her talking about Russ, who would be far more interesting if he was actually one of the undead, that she didn't nor would she ever think about me in terms of a boyfriend. And perhaps I didn't want her to make me her boyfriend anyway. I would just have to be a zombie or perform some other act of pain and humiliation while she laughed with her real friends, which at this point were Sarah, Erin, and me. But I would lose my place if I were her boyfriend. On one hand, we would have sex. But on the other hand I couldn't go out with her and laugh at some dumb idiot. If I were her boyfriend, I would be the dumb idiot.

Only I didn't think it through in this degree of detail. Other things distracted me. I went to class. On the way from class to my work in the stockroom at the bookstore, I noticed the girl I'd had in my German class, a stoner with very curly hair, who always wore t-shirts she made herself. They usually had some kind of cartoon on them. Today's was a man carrying an umbrella and another one walking in the rain and whistling. They were both stick figures. The whistle was indicated by little musical notes rising from his mouth. The man under the umbrella had slashes for eyes. He was not happy. "Where can I get a shirt like that?" I asked her.

"I make them," she said. It was, I might point out, obvious that she made them.

"Can I buy one?"

"I can give one to you," she said. "If you give me a shirt to make it on."

"I'll bring my shirt around this afternoon," I said. "Can I have one like yours?"

"I'd give you this one, but I'm wearing it," she said. And then she blushed. "And I'd need to wash it first."

"I don't think it would fit me," I said.

"Oh yeah," she said. "There's always that."

I thought about this girl who I had been buying coffee from every day for the last three weeks. Why had I not been able to think about her before?

I bought a t-shirt and took it back and gave it to her and then, oddly, we had a date to drink coffee so I could pick up my shirt. It seemed a bit redundant to make a date with someone who worked a coffee cart to go and drink coffee, but that's what I did.

I found myself on my bike riding down the paved trail that used to be a railroad when I was a child; we'd hike over the ties to collect blackberries. It was now a paved road with people rollerblading or couples picnicking on the nearby grass, eating humus and slices of tomatoes while siting on wool plaid blankets. Everyone was out in the sun, and not thinking about other things, or so it seemed to me. All of the pensive walkers and the people waving their arms and shouting at the sky were missing today. They were taking the day off, and only the people who wanted to have a good time were out and about today. And this was how I liked it. I was out riding my bike wearing my new t-shirt. I stopped in the shadow of the bridge and sat by the ship canal, full of dark blue water, with even darker blue stones tumbling down into the deep water of the channel. I would bring the coffee girl here, and we would have ourselves our own picnic on a wool blanket, but we would eat meat instead of whipped chickpea. We would eat fried chicken and cherries and drink red wine. We wouldn't eat tofu or soy, unless that is all she ate. I would eat tofu or soy for her.

On the way back to my car, I began to wonder about Laura. Was I so quickly finished with her? I didn't miss her so much because she was still my friend, although I could tell that once this tension had been removed between us, the likelihood of us finding each other interesting enough to even be friends was unlikely. I liked her, but I liked dozens of people I didn't hang out with every weekend. What kept me drawn to her was the tension that I was attracted to her and terrified to let her know a thing. I should just not call her.

However, Laura called me. If asked about this aspect of our friendship, I would say I was the one who always arranged things with her. I had believed it would be an easy matter of not doing anything, and we would drift apart. But she called. I said I would bring some gin and then that weekend the five of us were in her apartment again.

I brought the alcohol, a fifth of Bombay Sapphire and a plastic jug of clear rotgut. I figured this was it. If she even called again I would be busy with the coffee girl. We drank the nice gin in gentile company listening to the new album that Erin had brought and then after we finished the record, we made a pretense of eating. Russ had brought beer, damn him, and he drank that. I didn't think he would get zombie drunk again.

I wore my new t-shirt and like a dutifully nosy friend Laura asked where'd I'd picked it up.

"From this girl at the espresso cart near the bookstore," I said.

"What does she look like?" Laura asked.

"I can't describe people. She has curly black hair."

"Of course."

"She has pale skin."

"Yeah."

"When I see her, a theme song plays."

"What kind of song?"

"'I Need You'," I said. "The Troggs. It's a classic rock love story."

"Have you ever even had a girlfriend before?"

"Yeah," I said. I mean there had been girls, and we went out and did stuff. I don't know whether it was like boyfriend girlfriend kind of stuff. "Oh yeah," I said again. I didn't want to say I'd been distracted since I met her.

After Russ had three beers, he had a shot of the nice gin and that pushed him nicely over into the land of the living dead. Laura was pleasantly drunk as well, and then I asked her if she could make us all zombies and she did, she dressed us up as zombies, and while she was working on us, we finished the nice gin and moved into the rotgut. I didn't want to drink it, but I had a shot with Russ, and then I began to shoot glasses of water to his glasses of gin and pretty soon we were all zombies.

That is, we were as close as we could come to zombies without actually ripping our clothes. Zombies in the movies never really had the smell of zombies either. I imagine in real life the smell of a zombie would be more distinctive than their look. We left our clothes disheveled, but no one actually ripped anything. And we didn't smear ourselves with rotting meat.

"What's her name?" Laura asked.

"Ashley," I said. "But she goes by Ash."

"Of course. How gothic," Laura said. "You like Ash the Goth."

"Hey," I said, "Let's go somewhere as zombies." We climbed down to my car, an old Duster that my mother had given me to visit her in Enumclaw. We drove in the Duster to Green Lake, a packed park even at night, and then we shuffled out of the car as zombies. We shuffled in the darkness, and we passed some people. They were amused. Russ shouted, "Must eat brains!" His voice was garbled and broken from the gin. He ran after them. They laughed, but didn't run.

I wanted to shout to them, "Run for your lives!" but that wouldn't have been very zombie of me.

Russ lunged forward. We could see his face drop into some guy's chest.

"He bit me!" The guy's voice cracked. His friends, rather than staying to protect him, ran.

Russ ran after them. The guy he bit lay on the ground. We shuffled toward him, remaining in zombie character. I wondered if we should comfort him. The guy seemed very upset. But he saw us shuffling and then he lifted himself up and off he ran.

"Where did Russ go," Erin asked. "Where did that freak go?"

He returned from the bushes. He didn't have his clothes on again, and he had his big old flag up.

"Oh Christ," I said. There were the lights of a police car at the other side of the lake. We ran back to the Duster and drove to the apartment. We waited in the dark parking lot.

"Where are your clothes?" I asked Russ.

"Zombie," he said.

"If you bite me," I said. "I'll sock you in the head."

"Zombie," he said.

We went inside and as soon as we stepped into the apartment Russ fell asleep on the floor. He had blood on his face that was real blood in addition to the fake blood that Laura had colored on him. We sat in the darkness unable to fathom what had just happened. As we sat there it seemed like something that maybe hadn't really happened. To me, it seemed like a sure way of getting sick with something. If a person got salmonella from eating raw chicken, what would they get from raw human flesh?

"He's a pervert," I said to Laura.

"I know," she said. "Takes one to know one."

"What do you mean you know?"

"It doesn't bother me. Secretly I kind of like it."

"It's not a secret if you're telling me."

"I put zombie makeup on him last night. Zombie love is not for everyone."

"It is a fact," I said, citing something from my anthropology class, "All cultures in the world find the blemish ugly."

"His erection doesn't go away when he is a zombie."

"That's necrophilia."

"The makeup is not real, but his erection is real."

"What do you mean?"

"It won't go away."

"Doesn't that bother you?"

"Why should that bother me? When I'm tired of it I can wipe off his makeup. But, it is there if I want it."

"I like it when I don't know what people are going to do," I said.

"To each his own," Laura said. I'd heard that, but I didn't know what it meant. To each his own what?

When I woke in the apartment, Russ was gone. Sarah and Erin had taken the bed in the bedroom. I slept on the couch, and someone had wrapped me in a blanket.

"Where's Russ?" I asked.

"He had to go to work." He worked part time in a lumber store.

"I made you breakfast," she said. "Erin and Sarah are still asleep," she said.

"Thank you."

"So what shall we do today?" she asked me.

"What do you mean?"

"Why don't we do something? I mean after we fix our headaches. What were you going to do with that girl today? Do it with me instead."

"What about Russ?"

"He's a zombie."

I didn't say anything until after I had my coffee and ate some aspirin and drank a tumbler of water. I looked at myself in the hallway mirror, and I was as white as the dead. She stood in the hallway close enough to me that even after drinking all of that gin, after chasing people down in the park as zombies, she still smelled pretty. "Well?" But it was too late. I'd been her pet already and even though this is what I'd wanted, I just shrugged. I didn't know what she was even asking me. "I have some things I have to do today," I said. "Maybe another time," I said. I said the things I normally would say so that I could leave. "I'll call you later," I said. She stood in the window watching me back the Duster out of the driveway. I waved to her and she waved, dropping her fingers against the windowpane.

Crossing Sunday Creek

I met RedHawk the first time I was in the woods. I'd lost my car. I'd heard of idiots who lost their car before, but I didn't think I'd ever be one. I'd always thought they were drunk. It's not like the woods are a parking lot. When you park your car, it's the only one there, but I couldn't even find the road. Welts and damp cotton covered my skin. I didn't want to sleep in the forest, although I'd already thought about how I might find a dry place to spend the night under the boughs of a cedar tree. I didn't even want to think of the bugs that might be living under there: millipedes the width of Twinkies. I was starting to panic when I found this guy snoozing on a cedar trunk. The tree hung over a wild stream. He lay on the silver bark.

He didn't have on shoes, and he snored faintly. He could have been asleep there for an hour, for three hours, for thirty years. If I woke him up and we went back to the city together he'd look around and ask "Since when did every other person on the road stop driving a Chevy?"

Everywhere else in the forest it was raining. This guy was sleeping in what seemed like the only spot of sun in the entire woods. His sleeping there made it seem like the forest was hospitable. Myself, I felt as if I might die there. You read about guys losing their way in the forest all the time. Just last year some guy went the wrong way and ended up living for four days on lichen. His feet got frostbite, so they cut off his toes. The whole time he was about five miles from Interstate-90. He might as well have been in Siberia for all the good it did him. Happens all of the time.

I thought at first that RedHawk, himself, was one of these victims. He'd died out there. He didn't stir when I came out of the forest, even though I made a ton of noise. The stems of bushes snapped: rocks skittered and fell down the bank into the stream. Steam came off me in clouds. I brushed the cool water off my face and let the sun warm my skin and I stood there for a second looking at him. He looked completely at peace, as if he lived there. He opened one eye to look at me. Then he closed his eye. I wasn't sure if he had seen me or if he'd just stirred. I turned, and then suddenly I heard this crash and he was standing behind me with the biggest knife I've ever seen up close. It had a nasty section of teeth. It was polished and turned gold in the sunlight.

"Tell me who you are before I kill you for trespassing," he said.

"My name is Derek," I said.

"Derek?" he repeated. "I'm RedHawk," he said.

I looked at him. He had reddish hair. He had nearly albino white skin with tiny, pink colored freckles. He had a bit of a paunch, but otherwise he looked really buff. I don't think in a fight, even without the knife, that I could take him. He was taller, too.

"Are you going to kill me?" I asked him. I realized he could. There was nothing to prevent that from happening. I could die, and he could bury me in the forest and no one would ever find me.

RedHawk looked at me then and I think he realized that was the case, too. He could kill me. I hoped that an adrenalin rush would come to help me, but nothing did.

We were on the lip of the bank already, but I didn't think about it. He leaned toward me with his hand out, and I was so jumpy, I jumped backwards. I was in the air and for a split second I thought I would plunge into the depths of the river.

RedHawk grabbed me. He jerked me back onto the bank. I scrambled onto the edge, kicking down a cascade of rocks, ferns, and dirt. I scrambled up the loose fill and then stood in the trees where RedHawk had been lying peacefully before I had come along.

"Derek," he said. "You are one high-strung dude."

That was how I met RedHawk. He had some beer in his pack and we spent the rest of the afternoon drinking the beer and looking out at the rain falling in the forest around us but marveling at our spot of dry and sun. At dusk, we went downstream to a place where the river widened out and we could walk on rocks without getting too wet. We crossed the swamp in the twilight and then got into our cars. RedHawk drove an old Celica from the 1980s, a tiny car that was rusted in a uniform, earthy brown. I couldn't believe he could fit into the car, but he sat down, and then he was inside it and he waved with his fingers all spread apart.

We began to go into the mountains almost every weekend. Usually, we went from the Sunday Lake trailhead up to wherever we could from there. I loved those mountains because they were beyond all of the crap in the city. Usually, I felt like people knew me because of the car I drove, the clothes I wore, the job I did. Out there none of that applied. The washed-out roads and the swamp kept most people out and the people we did meet tended to be survivalist types like us. Often, we'd get there and there wouldn't be anyone for the entire weekend. Or sometimes we would stop and discover tracks, but they only told us where not to go.

Before this, to be honest, I had not thought much about the mountains that I could always see from Seattle. To me a tree was a tree, a stick with leaves. I knew there were trees that didn't lose their leaves and that was about it. For RedHawk, each tree had a name and a purpose and in the forest we began to learn there were special trees, individual trees that RedHawk had a special relationship with.

I learned that RedHawk had to be someone else in the

city as well. Gradually, during those months of hiking in the forest as the summer turned into fall and then the snow fell, I learned he was named Pete Gorse, and that he worked in a warehouse in Bothell near 405. Bothell was a thriving suburb filled with Boeing Engineers and software types from Bellevue. When I was growing up, it had always been depressed, but now it was full of fancy condo strip malls, luxury grocery stores, and office parks filled with warehouses. My father had bought land in Lynwood before I was born, and he had a picture on his dresser of the gigantic stumps on his land. Each individual stump was bigger than he was.

Pete was fired from his job and then got another job. He was always coming up with ways his workplaces could improve their business. When he started a job, he said, the first thing he figured out was how they could do the job better. Then, he started to do it better. The problem is, he said, usually the reason he can do the job better is because the management sucks.

That winter he got a job as an actual manager and, for a while, he stopped going hiking with me, just as things started to get interesting. "Be careful," he said over coffee one night, "what you wish for."

In November, he got away one weekend and in the first snow he showed me how to snowshoe. We tramped our way up to a secluded valley where bears lived. RedHawk said it was safe because they were hibernating. We came to a stand of pine trees with huge bell-shaped bases, and in the middle of them there was a shelter. It had maybe been a miner's cabin or something fifty years ago, but now it had been adopted by people like RedHawk. "This is my camp," he said.

The shelter sat in the middle of these crazy pine trees. Their bark was thick, and I could only describe them as scabby. They went for about a quarter of a mile and then all sides of the canyon went straight up into the snow pack. It was about a mile of loose stones. Some of these gigantic stones had tumbled down into the valley, but nothing had hit the cabin. The cabin itself was on a little hill, so the rocks would have to fall and then roll up. It was somewhat warm in the canyon, being out of the wind.

RedHawk lit a fire and then he asked me whether I would like to choose my trail name. "We are different people out here," he said. "We are better than we are in the city. Out here, we are as we are supposed to be."

I didn't know what to say to this. I had thought his trail name was dorky, but I had never told him this because if he wanted to play Cowboys and Indians, more power to him, and when he explained what it was, it was even dorkier to be honest, but I also somewhat liked being someone else. "How about Tomahawk?"

"Tomahawk?" he said. "No that won't work because I'm RedHawk."

It kind of stung to have my name rejected. If we were going to be outdoor geeks, better go the distance I figured.

"BlackJack?" I said.

"I like that," he said, and it was my name. I didn't like it as soon as I said it because it made me sound like his sidekick. I'd do his dirty work for him, but no one else would ever know the name.

After that trip, though, RedHawk became immersed in his city life. He said he'd become management, and he could make some of his ideas come true. He talked about his job when I met him for coffee from time to time. I tried to go hiking by myself, but it wasn't the same. There was no one to call me BlackJack.

A month later, RedHawk called me in the middle of the week. "I'm out of here, man," he said. "I made the mistake of putting my identity into it, and that never works out right," he said.

"How's the job?"

"That's what I'm talking about. When you get a chance, BlackJack, you come and pay me a visit at the base."

After work I drove by his apartment, but it was dark. His Celica wasn't in the parking lot of his building.

I wondered if he'd taken enough food out there. At the store on Thursday I found myself daydreaming about living out there and I bought a bunch of heavy-duty staples: rice, potatoes, cut oats, jerky.

That weekend I drove out to the trailhead and there was his car. A layer of snow covered it. I put on my backpack and had to put on snowshoes right away. I crossed the stream. The water was nearly freezing and black compared to the caps of white snow on each of the individual rocks. It was pretty easy to cross Sunday Creek because the water was way down on account of the snow. The forest felt open now that it was covered in white snow. After about five hours, I finally arrived at the base. I realized then that the shelter was built in a kind of avalanche chute. The shelter sat on a hill, but all around it the snow went right up to the mountaintops. It was muffled and quiet in the valley. There was a huge fire burning near the shelter. It had melted all of the snow around the cabin. And RedHawk's stuff was in a tent inside of the shelter, but he wasn't anywhere. I would have called out, but I was afraid I'd set the avalanches off. I sat and listened to the crackling fire, then toward dusk I could hear him cursing as he came out of the darkness.

"BlackJack!" He carried a Safeway bag full of fungus and a couple of fish.

He sat down. "I'm having a hell of a time finding stuff to eat. I didn't bring enough grub."

I'd brought potatoes, steak, butter, pepper, carrots, oatmeal. When he saw what I'd brought he wiped his eyes. "I don't know if I'm ready, BlackJack. I've been studying what I need for survival, and I don't think there are enough calories out here for me to survive."

"This is just a place to come," I told him. "It would be kind of crazy to live out here. You'd be like one of those hermits in that TV show."

"What?"

"Monty Python. One of those guys who can't speak anything except gibberish and are wearing ragged clothes and have a crazy beard." RedHawk did have the beginning of a crazy beard.

"This has been the best four days of my life," RedHawk said. "I need to be out here. I don't want anything to do with that other person I am."

"Listen to yourself, man," I said. "You call yourself RedHawk. That is just a character. You are really that guy who works in a warehouse. You are Pete Gorse."

RedHawk didn't say anything. "Did you bring more food?"

I put the sack of potatoes, rice, and jerky on the boards of the cabin. "Come back in one month," he said. "If I can make it for a month out here, than this is where I belong."

"You're going to go crazy," I said. "Or freeze to death. Or something."

"Then I deserve to," he said.

I sat with him for a while and then set up my tent on the bare ground near the shelter. He left while I set up my tent, then he returned with a load of sticks he dropped in the fire. It sent up a shower of sparks, twirling black ash, and smoke. It wasn't desolate in the valley where he'd set up his base camp. The trees provided a kind of nice, park-like feeling. They were blunt and stunted from the boulders and avalanches that had crashed into them. The shelter did pretty much protect him from that kind of stuff. There was a stream that passed under us in the ice. He could get water if he needed it. We hardly talked that night. We ate our food, and then I took out my bottle of Jim Beam. "To life in the woods," I said. I wasn't sure if I felt jealous of RedHawk or not. I didn't think I could hack it, just living out there with nothing much to do but collect wood, try to find food, and let my mind eat itself. He had enough food now, though, that he would live at least until I came back in a month, should I be able come back. The weight of that responsibility began to sit on me and I hadn't even left yet. He could always walk back out, too. It wasn't far to his car, but, in a month his car might not run anymore, or hooligans might shoot it full of holes. Everything left on the sides of the county road was full of bullet holes. I didn't say anything about his Celica because I didn't want to take any kind of responsibility for it myself.

In the light of the campfire, it was as if we owned the entire world. I went out onto the ice and, away from the camp, there was enough light I could see. The world was easy to navigate now that it was covered in snow. In the summer it was all brush and creeks, but now it was just a flat expanse of snow. The white made it easy to see at night. The stars were above me. The fire was down in the valley. Could I exist with these as my only points of connection to the world?

RedHawk's fantasies often seemed pretty silly to me. The Cascades were just a park, really. They were an hour or two's drive away from a huge city. People came out to them on the weekend. That's how I got out there. At night, I could see the light of the city, but then I realized standing out there that I didn't see the light of the city. I was surrounded by forest, valleys, canyons, wild cataracts, caves, bears, coyotes, deer and so on for hundreds of miles. It went on for dozens of miles even before the clear cuts started. I could fit another entire state in the space between me and the city, an entire European country.

RedHawk woke me before dawn. He wanted to show me the hot springs. There was a well-known hot springs in the Middle Fork Valley, but he said there was another one here too. So I strapped on my snowshoes and packed my stuff, and we walked. He didn't carry a backpack because he was pretty much at home anyway. We crossed up to the top of the valley just as the day started to get light. There wasn't a dawn; rather, the darkness just began to get less intense. We crossed through a narrow pass, and then down into a warm pocket of forest where the snow wasn't very thick at all. The trees were huge. It was a patch of virgin growth in a valley stable enough to let the trees get to full size. In that mossy place there was a gravel stream and next to the stream there was a well that bubbled out scalding water. The water smelled of sulfur, odd minerals, and steam. We stripped and climbed into the water. The surface seemed incredibly hot and immersed in the roiling water, I could feel my muscles relax. My skin turned bright red. What more could a person need?

On the way back down, feeling now like I wanted to stay here myself, RedHawk gathered some mushrooms and some fungus he liked. It was kind of like a store.

"Why don't you live in this valley?" I asked.

"I like the other place," he said. "It's not a long walk up here and it gives me a place to go, something to do."

I left and, for the rest of that month, RedHawk was all I could think about, living away from the world like that. He could only do it, I realized, because of me. I also kept thinking I'd get a call from him, or I'd read the newspaper and he'd be dead. Or, when I finally got back out there, he would be dead. My work became a kind of joke. I thought of myself as a slave, as someone doing not what they should do because they could do it passably well, but because I was enslaved by a system designed to abuse me. I sat at night in my apartment hearing the sounds of people moving around in the apartments above me. I banged on the ceiling until the landlord came and told me to shut it down. At work my boss told me to wear an elf hat. It was the week before Thanksgiving. I kept working and set the elf hat on the counter, and then she said, "Derek, put the hat on now." I put it on, "Happy Holidays," I said.

I kept my word, though, and waited a month. I then loaded up on potatoes, whole oats, the kind of dry goods that a miner might have taken into the Cascades in the 1890s. I thought I might stay out there myself. Forget about my apartment filled with all of my crap. A warm rain had come from the Pacific during the holidays. The roads were wet, but I kept waiting to come to snow and even at the trailhead the precipitation was rain rather than snow. Nothing is as dismal as rain on snow.

The first bad sign was his car. It was now lying in the brush and had been mostly dismantled and filled with holes and the rusting fragments were covered in the snow.

The second bad sign was the creek that had become a massive torrent under the snow. Even the shallow fjord was now five feet of racing ice melt. I was weighed down with my stuff and couldn't just cross. I took everything off except my underpants, and then put my stuff in garbage bags and put it over my head and left on my boots. The water instantly cooled my skin and it felt like the river was made out of fire. I screamed and pushed the bundle of my stuff to the other bank, and then I scrambled to the top. My skin was bright red. I dried off quickly and stamped my feet and put on clothes. It felt fantastic: I wondered how I would get back across, but then realized I might not be coming back.

I began to hike in order to warm up and soon I was fine. The forest was easy to pass through because the snow had begun to pack in the last month. As I climbed the steep valley, the rain turned to snow, and the world turned back into the smooth ease of mid-winter snowpack. The shelter was empty. The fire pit was full of ashes and had been used since the last snow. I camped there that night and in the middle of the night I woke when something crashed into my tent.

I jumped out of my tent trying to find some kind of weapon. I had my flashlight, and I turned it on and was ready to hit whatever it was that had smashed into the tent. RedHawk had a full crazy beard and he stood with his legs apart and held a long, crooked branch.

"RedHawk?" I asked.

"BlackJack!" he said.

It was one of those moments that don't feel real even as you are having it. We embraced. He sat down. "I didn't think you'd come," he said. "Are you late?"

"Right on time, man," I said.

He ate and then puked and then ate some more, and then finally he slept. I woke in the morning, and he still slept. I gathered wood. When he woke I could see he had lost a lot of weight. He was oddly clean, and then I realized he must have been spending a lot of time in the hot springs.

"So how was it?" I finally asked after breakfast. He held his coffee cup and stared into it with admiration.

"Terrible and wonderful," he said. "I got so bored some days I wanted to crack my skull open. But, most of the time it was just me and my body out here. I felt as alive as a person can feel. I can't explain it."

"I brought some more food," I said.

"I need more than food," RedHawk said. "I need to get out of here," RedHawk said. "I need to see other people. All I've been able to think about out here is sitting in the mall. I want to shower and shave, put on some clean clothes and go and sit in a mall and listen to people talk to each other. I don't care if they don't see me. I don't care, but I can't take another week of ice and snow."

"But you are who you are supposed to be out here," I said. "We can be ourselves."

"Give me your keys, then," he said. "Let me have your car and apartment. You can stay here. I'm not going to stop you, BlackJack." He waved his hands in the air. "Have at it! It's yours."

We drank our Jim Beam. I walked out onto the ice and listened to the darkness of the mountains above us. Snow fell in heavy flurries. I could see the campfire, but that was it. Snow gathered on my shoulders. I felt the keys in my jeans pocket, the key to my apartment full of crap and my car. I'd just had the oil changed. I wasn't giving my stuff to this lunatic.

I didn't want to be out there for one more minute, but it was the middle of the night. "You can crash at my place," I told Pete Gorse, "Until you find a job and a place. You tried, man."

"Tomorrow I'm going to the mall," he said.

Knot

I was made of string. While walking on the sidewalk back from the beach where I went during my lunch to drink coffee from my thermos and look at the gulls, I was afraid I'd snag myself on a bush and I'd begin to unravel. I hooked myself on a blackberry or something. Blackberries grew in the margins between people's houses where they didn't pay attention, where anything growing could be the responsibility of the person next door, and no one wanted to cut what didn't belong to them. Of course, because of this fear I jinxed myself and this is exactly what occurred. I snagged myself on the brambles near the empty lot.

I was packed as a baseball is packed: a tiny round part, my bones, encircled with string around and around, tied and covered with skin. While I had not been paying attention during my morning walk around the block, muttering to myself about my equations and trying to remember what it was I was trying to prove and for whom, I wore a hole in my skin. I didn't apply a bandage. It scabbed and would heal, but on the walk that afternoon down to the beach under the clear winter sky I discovered the tide had come in bringing in seaweed and upended starfish. The starfish were wrapped in weeds and kelp. The starfish had more than just five arms. Some of them had six or eight or twelve arms. They were long and curled around their body in elaborate sweeps. They were orange and brown and russet. The gulls let out piercing cries as they hunted the helpless starfish. Each gull emitted a sound at a regular interval, and among other gulls, their cries overlapped and spread, creating a jarring, pulsing agitation that spread through the entire beach. I wasn't able to take my peaceful lunch and drink my coffee on the bay-side stones. In a panic, I picked the scab from my skin and exposed a loose fiber of string.

I tried to tuck it back in. I thought I had done so. If only I chewed gum, I could patch myself this way. If only I bicycled, I could patch myself with the repair kit.

When I snagged myself, the string began to come loose. I didn't notice it. The string is very thin. A person can hardly see it. A well-placed foot in fact can sever the string. I left a trail as thin as spider's silk from the blackberry bush into my house, and then through my house it followed me as I went about my day performing my calculations, fixing coffee, laying in the yard on the cool grass on my yoga mat and staring directly into the blue to empty my mind of everything except my problem.

I began to lose weight because it was trailing behind, a thin extension of myself. At first, I thought it was because I wasn't eating well. I tend not to eat well when I am working on a particularly intractable problem. I spoke to my mother on the phone, and she mentioned the flu at her work. She worked on a computer in what is called a server farm. It was just her, and the janitor in the server farm. Around them were farms that grew vegetables in the late summer. In the winter, the fields were covered with ice and snow. "You mean," I said, "the janitor is sick?" "People have something, and it is going around. Maybe you have that?" "Who?" I asked. "Mom, there is no nobody there." "There are people here. I'd be lonely if there weren't. Everyone's got a job," she said. "And right now a lot of them are home sick. I'd be lonely if I thought they weren't coming back." I ate more, but still I kept becoming smaller and smaller. At first, I liked the sensation of being small and sitting at my desk. I moved more freely, and then I began to notice the string of myself sticking to well-trafficked locations.

I inspected myself and found the spot that hadn't healed. Lepers do not feel such things, and I wondered if I had this disease. I didn't want to go the doctor to find out because he most likely would be puzzled to discover I was made of string. I patched myself then with a band-aid. I cleaned the house with a bucket, solvent, and a specially purchased rag because I do not keep rags in the house. The houses needed a good rub down anyway.

At the beach the next day I couldn't think about my problem. Instead, I wondered, how did I come to be made of string? Other animals are not made of string as far as I know. I was made from scratch like a doll by mother; my bones carefully wrapped in gossamer until I had muscle and flesh and brain. My equation seemed trivial after such a realization.

Hunger

Early one morning before I was awake, she leaned over to bite the tip of my index finger. She snapped the tip of my index finger off in her mouth like a piece of chocolate. Before I bled she held her thumb again the stump. The shock was so great I went from being completely asleep to awake and I trembled in the bed unsure of what had just happened, and she soothed me as tears came to my eyes. What had happened, I wondered now, awake and grateful to have her in bed with me. I felt better at once and felt in fact better than I normally felt as I suppose adrenalin and other substances coursed through me. The faintly blue light of before dusk permeated the room. I could hear a car idling a few houses down. My son murmured in his sleep in his bedroom down the hall. Lindsey was not a stranger to me. We had been dating for two years. I still eagerly anticipated our evenings together when we went out to eat dinner at some restaurant our foodie of a friend recommended to us, or we stayed in and watched DVD movies. We typically kept to the house when my son was over. She got along with him. During the night I sometimes woke to hear her snoring gently. She slept in one of my t-shirts. She pressed her lips to mine and kept her hand pressed against my hand and then in the morning when I woke I found my finger neatly wrapped. "Let it rest," she said. "I will be out of town." This was written in her impeccable hand on a piece of stationery and folded into a letter on my side table.

I cooked an egg and drank my black coffee. I pondered what had happened to my finger. Surely she had not bitten my finger in the middle of the night and then repaired it without my knowledge? During the day my finger ached and I had difficulty typing on the keyboard. I wondered then if I had done something. It had been a number of years since I drank heavily. I had not actively stopped drinking, but rather noticed that when I did not drink I felt better and so gradually the impulse to drink was replaced by an impulse not to drink because when I drank I felt tired and sluggish the next day. In the days when I did drink though, I drank whatever I could get my hands on and once, for instance, I woke to find myself in bed and the last thing I remembered was drinking at a hotel in the mountains many miles from home. A different car was in the driveway. I suppose I was lucky because I never killed anyone. I never maimed myself through carelessness. To say carelessness implies I had some degree of awareness while drunk. I exited from my body and when I returned someone else had been using it, and it could easily have lost a limb, an arm, and a finger. But a part of a finger? This loss placed me into the same state of mind and I had no idea how it had come to pass that I had lost this portion of a digit.

I scheduled an appointment with my doctor. I learned to cope with the shorter finger. Lindsey called from her trip. She was vice president of a business intelligence-consulting firm. She articulates the discipline of business intelligence. She was zealous in her corporation and was still young by corporate standards. Likely she would be a president by fifty and would move on. Her first husband had been a high school football star who ran his own drywalling business. Her second husband had been a professor at her college. After she left him she said there was no point in marrying. She met me in a German class. Although she couldn't attend, she would have me conference her by cell phone and she would listen from some distant location— Madrid, Manila, Prague. I didn't learn to speak the language even though I carefully studied the tape, and used flash cards, and went to the extra conversational German sessions. Lindsey, though, learned German because she was speaking German with Germans and she aced the final test. I passed, but by passing I was aware I would never be fluent in German.

When she was in town, she stayed at her condo on the water near my house. She came over to sleep the night. I don't know how well I knew her. She had talked at length

about her first and second husbands. She got along well
with my son. Generally she was at the end of email, chat, or
a distant and static-filled cell phone connection. I suppose
I liked this: her being temporary. I had her now and she
had me and we didn't have to consider other aspects of
our life together. We didn't have to wonder where it would
be going because it was clear this was it. She was going
to be a president, and I would be the father of a son who
had graduated from high school. I would be a man who
did jobs to pay for his car loan and mortgage and on the
weekends, when she was out of town and my son was with
his mother, I would go for long walks along the defunct
railroad beds and stop at the edge of a marsh and stare into
the putrid water where the brown and gray water met the
gray and blue sky. In short, I was a person who experienced
life and had long ago given up on the imperative that it
had to lead somewhere. Eventually you arrive somewhere.
I had arrived there.

This arrival wasn't necessarily happiness. It wasn't stasis
or limbo either. I read a book about behavior modification
and this book talked about washing dishes. Typically,
people who do dishes want to finish doing the dishes,
this book said. They do the dishes but are really thinking
about not the dishes but what they will do after they do
the dishes. The book explained that to achieve peace is to
occupy the task of doing the dishes. Think about what you
are doing while you do it. Enjoy doing the dishes because
you are doing the dishes. Enjoy reading because you are
reading. And so on.

And this is how I felt about my life now. The other

things that had been present in my life, the striving I had or ambition or what have you when I was younger, had faded or stalled if I looked at it from the point of view of myself as I was when I was 25. At 25, say, I would have been disgusted by myself. I had been miserable at 25.

I learned to enjoy having a slightly shorter index finger.

The doctor took off the bandage. He examined it. "Do you have the rest of the finger?"

"What do you mean?"

"If you had the tip of your finger we could probably have fixed your finger. But it is too late now. If this ever happens again—which I'm sure it won't—but if it ever happens again you should get the rest of the finger put on ice and come to the emergency room as quickly and as safely as you can."

"How did this happen?" he asked me.

"I was asleep..." I said.

"Do you drink?"

"No," I said.

"This would have been very painful. It would have been something you couldn't have slept through. How did you get this bandage."

"My wife—rather, girlfriend—applied it."

The doctor examined the finger. "It's healing. There is nothing we can do."

And so my life proceeded for some time and then one night while sleeping with Lindsey in the bed, I woke. She held my finger. She had bitten another joint off my index finger. "Hush, sweetheart," she said.

"Where is it?" I asked. "Where is my finger?"

"It is right here," she said and she gently squeezed my hand, sending an electrical pulse of pain through my body.

"I need to get to the emergency room and they can fix it."

"They wont be able to do anything," Lindsey said.

"Where is my finger?"

"I chewed it up and swallowed it, silly," she said, and she pecked me on the cheek. She had come back from Europe with fantastic perfume and I smelled it while she hugged me.

"There is no finger?" I asked.

"There is no finger," she said.

I wanted to get out of bed then. Why was she eating me? Is that what was going on? She made love to me even though I was half awake and I didn't budge. I felt oddly great and weirdly removed.

In the morning I didn't think about it. I made do with the stub that was now my right-hand index finger. There was no point in going to the doctor and gradually I didn't think about it. Lindsey was out of town. My son spent the summer in a camp and the loss of my fingers became a regular occurrence. At first I had some 28 units and gradually they dwindled. When the last one was gone, I cried. "What are you going to do now, Lindsey?" I asked.

"Your arms are too big for me to eat," she said.

"My toes."

"I don't eat feet," she said.

In the morning in her neat handwriting she left a note. She thanked me for the years I had provided for her. She said she would miss me, but there was nothing left for her.

The Princess Bed

After our daughter was born, my wife and I bought her a child-sized bed, a princess sleigh bed made out of heavy wood, painted white. Curved rails ran along the headboard and foot. It was a really solid bed. It was very comfortable. We also bought a crib that attached to the side of our own bed so that my wife wouldn't have to get out of bed, go to the our daughter's room where I thought the baby would sleep, and breastfeed her. It saved my wife from getting out of the bed. It saved me from getting out of bed. But during the night, our baby ended up in our bed. I didn't have any room. One night I moved to the then unused princess bed. I slept soundly.

After I started to sleep in the princess bed, I liked

sleeping in the bed. I would get a sound night's sleep, which I needed because I had to get up in the morning and work construction. I started the work because I knew a guy who got me a job at a site. After that I liked the money, but the work wore me out. To be tired at the site was dangerous. Anything could happen if I was tired at the site. Tired guys did things like drop hammers. They sheared off their fingers. I was glad to get a full night's sleep even though my wife hardly ever got a full night's sleep. Our daughter kept her awake.

At first the baby went to sleep late. She had day and night reversed. She slept during the day and just as we lay down to sleep for the night, she was ready to play. We worked out a system where we would put her to bed in the sidecar crib fifteen minutes earlier every single night. After a few weeks my wife and I could have some time together before I turned in to the princess bed and she turned in, in the bed next to the baby.

It wasn't an ideal situation, but it worked okay. Our daughter woke through the night. She breastfed and my wife became so good at it, she hardly woke. For the most part my wife slept. Myself, I slept well once I went out. The princess bed was well made. It was a solid piece of furniture. The best bed I ever slept in, really. I continued to sleep in the bed even as our daughter began to get older and less fussy. It was a big moment when the baby ate her first solid food. It was a big moment when she said her first word: cat. You'd think she would say "momma," but it was "cat," and then "bird," "hi," "rock," and then finally, "Momma." She was still breastfeeding then. We read that it was healthful to breastfeed for as long as possible. She kept to her schedule until she was three years old. By that time she was mostly toilet trained, but we were working through that. We talked about my wife and I moving back into our own bed again sometime, but it was always after the next thing in our daughter's development. She needed to become fully toilet trained.

I suppose there was a gap between her finally using the toilet and then her having night terrors where we could have easily made the transition back to my wife and I sleeping in the same bed. To be honest, by this time I was entrenched in the princess bed. I didn't really have a lot of incentive to sleep in the same bed as my wife. I slept soundly. We were never ones to get into hanky panky while sleeping. When I went to sleep, I went right to sleep and woke a minute before my alarm went off, unless I'd had something to drink the night before, or was coming down with something. I'd read that people with sleep disorders had to train themselves not to do other things in bed, like watch TV, or read books, or do their bills, or whatever. I never had that problem. When I lay my head down for the night, it was for one thing only, to sleep. So I guess that is why it never occurred to me that it was odd as year after year went by and I never moved out of my daughter's bedroom and back into my spot beside my wife. Instead my wife and daughter slept in one bed, I slept in the sturdy white bed with sleigh rails.

My wife was on hand to deal with the various sleep issues that came up with her daughter. After this brief window when she had learned to go to the bathroom herself, no longer breastfed, she began to experience night terrors. My wife woke our daughter a couple of hours after she went to bed to take her to the bathroom, and that kind of worked. Then she entered a long period of time, a period of time she only now at seven seems to be getting over where she wets the bed. We make sure she doesn't drink a lot of juice or soda or whatever before bed. It works most of the time, but not all of the time.

Our daughter was seven years old and still sleeping with my wife and I was still sleeping in our daughter's bedroom. It really seemed like her bedroom. She played in the rec room. We kept her toys in her room, but she rarely played in there.

One night I woke and thought my wife had come to visit in the night. It was fantastic. I am, I have to admit, a little lazy in that department and it was as if I had been used like a trampoline or a pogo stick or some kind of device used to propel a body into the air, repeatedly. I was bruised. I rubbed my wounds the next day, and after we put our daughter to bed in my wife's bed I said, "About last night..."

"I am so tired," she said.

"I think I'll have to skip the movie tonight. I bet you're tired after last night." She looked at me. She was playing dumb. If she wanted to play dumb, that was fine with me as long as it happened again sometime soon.

Again, she visited me in the middle of the night. Only this time I wanted to see her and leaned over to flick on the lamp and as soon as I did, she wasn't there. It was as if I was alone in the bed where a second before I had surely not been alone. Wanting to catch my wife before she went back to bed, I hurried into her room and she was still in bed. She lay as if she hadn't moved from before she fell asleep. "Honey," I said. "Come back."

"What are you talking about?"

"Come on," I said.

"As if that has ever worked, buster," she said. "Come on? Am I some kind of animal? Why don't you just get the broom and roust me out of bed so you can do it."

I was shocked. I thought about it though. The state I was in, whatever would work, if it would work, would be fine by me.

"I'm just trying to get you into a different bed," I said.

"Forget about it tonight," she said. "I am asleep."

I went back to bed and slept. I didn't know what to think. I was grumpy the next day and tired from having spent most of the night fuming. When I returned from work that night, I went to bed early. Again she visited me in the night. At one point, I said, "Why are you doing this?" I was joyful and frustrated at the same time. "Be quiet," my wife said from the next room. "You'll wake Susan." My wife said this from the next room.. "What is going on?" I thought. Whoever or whatever I was doing it with was gone. I didn't know what to think about this. I lay in the bed and the next night nothing happened. I was glad about that. I thought if it was some kind of bizarre psychosomatic condition, then it was probably for the best that I had snapped out of it. But after a week, I was thinking, what's so wrong with psychosomatic conditions if that is the result? Finally I was visited again in the middle of the night. I didn't say anything. I didn't try to rock the boat—no pun intended. It went on this way for many months. When my wife and I had an occasion to have sex ourselves and all it was nice but it wasn't anything compared to the acrobatics of my condition.

I had the sense there was a body. And then I felt in those months a firmness in the belly of this body. Imaginary or not it was a pregnant body. I had remembered this from before our daughter was born, the firmness and solidity of her pregnant belly. Naturally, that freaked me out. I jumped out of bed. I would have screamed. I turned on the light and there was nothing there. I went to the kitchen and drank a glass of water. I returned to my wife's bed.

"What are you doing?" my wife asked me. "You'll wake Susan."

"I just want to sleep," I said. I slept on the corner of their bed for several weeks. Sometimes when I woke in the middle of the night I thought I could hear someone singing a song, a lullaby. Sleep sweet baby.

The Tin Nose Shop

He had nothing to do, having already finished all the nothings that he learned to pass the time. He'd practiced writing the letter to his cousin again. He described the clouds over the wasteland. It was the only thing he could bear to describe. He didn't want to write to her about the other men in his unit. They were coarse and talked endlessly about the women they had fornicated with while on leave, before they left for the Continent, and what they would do once they returned home. At first, Martin doubted their stories. He ascribed to them the symptoms of a fantasy life resulting from their impoverished childhoods, their crowded schools, their lack of learning, and only when he went on leave to the muddy village near the sea where they promptly visited the brothel filled with local woman who were nearly bald, scabby, and broken from the rough handling of the soldiers, did Martin realize that they weren't boasting; in fact, Martin lived in another world at home. He joined the Army because of *Morte d'Arthur* and Arthur Rackham's improbable drawing of armor. A soldier to him seemed to be someone who may die, but death was like getting knocked down during a football match. You would hop right back up again. Most men, he reasoned, were like the Knights of the Round Table, jolly and polite and quick to get into a rough bit of trouble. Instead, he found during training that they swore. They didn't read books. They didn't read the newspaper even. They learned things by asking each other and relating the most improbable theories. They mostly watched each other do whatever it was they needed to do on the sly. They always tested one another to see who was stronger. The first weekend in the barracks, the men began to wrestle. Martin wrestled and managed to defeat a few of his fellow soldiers until a very short, thin man with broad shoulders who looked like a spider monkey managed to pin Martin against the polished barracks floorboards. Still, the men wrestled until, like a pack of animals, there were only two men left, the thin man with wide, angular shoulders and bunched up arms. He had his shirt off, and his trousers rolled. Another man still wore his shirt. He was huge. His arms were as thick as other men's legs. His legs were as thick as their torsos. His middle section was a knot of muscle. He picked up the little guy and flung him to the ground, but the little guy didn't even hit the ground but wrapped himself around the big man, and they grunted and wheezed as they struggled. They struggled for hours. Neither would cede to the other. Finally, in the dark, exhausted, the big guy fell down and the little guy, unable to defeat the big one but completely able to wear him out, declared victory. There was hardly anyone left to see it. Martin sat on his bunk reading his book, and he didn't even look up, not wanting to give the satisfaction to the little guy for enduring the match for so long. The ranking that had been worked out continued to inform the unit even after they were broken up and sent to fill out another company. In each company, the ghost of the sorted order continued to exist and the men toward the top remained at the top among the older soldiers. It was funny to Martin when he actually thought about it now. The older soldiers were merely a few weeks or even months "older" than them. In those few months, they had waited and moved from one location to another. Finally, they were all moved *en masse* to fill trenches recently cut into the enemy land.

Martin spent his time drawing his cousin's face from memory instead of writing her the letter he couldn't formulate. He wasn't certain if the face he drew really belonged to her, or if his fumbling attempts to make marks on the page randomly made an image and he was so hungry for an idea of her that he willfully believed it looked like her. Maybe he didn't even know what she looked like? He thought he might find a smudge on the trench walls and this would look like her, like those people in Asia discovering the Virgin Mary in a slice of bread. It said more about the people looking for these things then it did about the objects themselves. Anyone could see what he wanted to see. Martin didn't want the men in his platoon to see what he was working on. They had drawn female images on their gear. A mermaid twisted over one man's canteen. Her cetacean breasts narrowed to the areolas like the snout of a humpback. Tattoos of flowers resembled female privates. Their arms were decorated with obscene wallpaper. Martin folded the paper and placed it in his pocket before anyone could see what he had drawn. They invariably bragged about their exploits. He couldn't tolerate them saying, "Core, I'd like to get a bit of that." He couldn't have his poorly drawn memory of her incorporated into some inept fantasy.

"What's that you got there?"

"Nothing," Martin said.

At first, Martin couldn't believe the place they were in—a vast stretch of bald earth with a single tree trunk that resembled a broken stick. There was nothing other then the muck between the trenches and the echo of machine gunfire from a distant location either behind or in front of their position. Above Martin, cumulonimbus moved over their lines casting cool shadows. He waited for three weeks. Each day he woke and ate the tack they handed out with tea. He drank from his tin cup. Around ten o'clock he took his first drink of gin in the same cup, mixed with the dregs of his tea, sour milk, and particles of tea leaves. The gin tasted the way a motor engine lubricant smelled. After that he could no longer taste the gin. He stayed tight most of the day. Martin was glad to have things blunted, and then after three weeks he was unsure if he wanted to spend his time loitering in a trench that was already a grave. Everyone there had never been in the trench before. In the middle of the night, he woke. Explosions shook the other side, and then machine guns began their rolling beat like someone beating a drum with the spokes of a driving wheel. A group of men marshaled them and coaxed them down the line. Runners distributed boxes of ammunition and more gin. They began to fire. Though it was the middle of the night the sky was bright, silver, emptied of color, and softness, just darkness, and light, the clouds margins of white against the black of the sky. Objects burst in dark pops, invisible except for their aftermath of sparks and tracers. Along the ground, shapes moved from the other trench toward them. Martin aimed and fired, and he wondered if he stopped some of the shapes moving. He aimed, and then the shape seemed to melt into the ground. He couldn't tell whether he was the one making them fall. They spent the night aiming and firing and loading their weapons. The shapes never managed to get far. It was light, he realized, and he didn't know how it suddenly became light or if he had fallen asleep and woke when it was light. Or if it had been light before and he was just now aware it was light. The empty land between their trench and the other was full of objects now. There were bodies in the drab uniforms of the enemy. One of them had almost made it to the stick lodged in the mud that looked as if it might have been a tree once. That shape was a champion. The shape should get recognition, Martin thought, a big star, a monument, a national holiday where people in university could sleep in.

Martin ate his breakfast of tack and tea and drank his

ration of gin first thing. He slept not certain if he had been asleep before. He heard from one of the men he'd trained with that they would go up that night and gain the ground the enemy had lost by trying to take their position.

"Why don't we go now?" Martin asked.

"In broad daylight? Are you mad? They'll kill us all."

Martin wondered if it made a difference. The night would be as bright as day when they made their assault. Because nothing had happened for weeks no one really seemed that concerned that they would do anything that night. Martin slept in his spot, and then a sergeant placed his hand on the back of his neck. "Get into position, son," he said. The sergeant was no older than Martin. He might have been younger. But Martin was no sergeant. Martin shuffled with the other soldiers down the line. He knew they were in trouble when they gave them twice the ration of gin. The fist splash, they waited. "Drink it down." The second, they poured a good amount. Martin didn't have any trouble finishing it even if it tasted like the lubricant of a motor engine.

They jumped into the forbidden zone between the trenches. Martin made his way to the tree. And before he knew it the sky turned bright. He could see the clouds again. He ran for cover not toward his trench where he wasn't allowed but toward the enemy trench where he could gain cover and maybe find a place where he only had to worry about bayonets, fists, things that might not kill him outright. Around him, there was a deafening roar.

He woke when it was bright again. He didn't feel wounded. He felt calm as he had not felt for months. He felt calm as he did during Christmas break in his last year of school. For a second he thought he was about to see his cousin's face but she was gone before he could take note of her features. He realized he lay in something made out of fabric. A tent flapped in the breeze. There was a breeze, and the clouds still made their way above him through the blue sky with white streaks. Several birds drifted far above his position. He smelled an odor like the gin. He realized he could only see things from one eye. He could not lift his head. It was maybe strapped to a board.

He wondered if he had killed the enemy? He didn't feel inclined to talk or move his muscles. He lay in this position for many hours. The sky grew dark. In the darkness, a shape leaned over him and placed fluid he could not taste in his mouth. And then, Martin slept because he could do nothing else. When he woke he watched the clouds as he had been watching them all along. He tried to compose the letter to his cousin that he been trying to compose. But he could not think of anything besides, "the clouds are fluffy and very clean, very white."

When he woke again he woke because of a pain in his bowels. His entire body shook, and above him there was canvas and beside him, although he couldn't turn to examine it well, there was wood painted green. Something happened in his body, and he felt better and after he thought better of writing the letter to his cousin about clouds, he fell asleep again. He would think of other things to say.

He woke. He lay in a bed. He could feel the sheets with his feet. He realized when he was in the bed that he was wounded. He didn't know before what had happened to him. He was wounded, and he could hardly move. He could move his feet, though, and the sheets, real laundered sheets, were so completely perfect that he kept moving his feet. Finally, he lifted his head from the bed. There was something wrapping his entire head, his neck, his shoulder. He had the use of one hand, an elbow. And in this extension outward of elbow (check), arm (check), hand (check), fingers (check) he realized he was cataloging only one half of his body. One eye worked, and the other eye didn't seem to exist, much less work. He lay in one bed in a row of beds in columns of beds. It was like morning formation. The beds were full, and everyone stared at the ceiling. At the end of his row, a nurse read a book. She placed it down under the light, placing it face down to mark the place, a habit that would lead to the broken spine of the book, and came toward him. She stopped at the foot of his bed and checked something attached to the frame.

"Private Bates?"

"Yes, ma'am," Martin said. When he spoke he wondered if the left side of his face was numb.

"Are you in pain?"

"I don't think so, ma'am," he said. He was in the opposite of pain. If only he could feel the left side of his face then he would know it was there. If only he could feel pain in his eye, he would know it was there.

"Are you thirsty?" she asked.

He was thirsty. He could use the rotgut gin as well. "I am," he said.

She went back to the end of the row and returned with a cup. Martin reached out. In the tin, he could see himself in a fun house reflection. He realized he must look like a mummy. His head was wrapped completely. The left side of his body was in plaster. It was tricky to drink from the cup, but he managed to pour the water in his mouth and swallow. He drank the contents of the cup.

"You are in hospital," she said.

"Where am I?"

"Normandy," she said. "When you are well enough, the doctors will fix you up proper."

Something about the way she said this made him wonder. She didn't say it with any level of conviction. "Proper" is what you might say to someone who was left down wrong. He didn't know how to ask her the truth of the matter. He knew in the way she said this that she wasn't telling him the truth or that the truth wasn't something she could tell him. She didn't know the truth.

He had waited for weeks to get blown up, if that is what had happened to him. He could wait for weeks for them to put him back together again. If the King's Horses could put an egg back together, trained medical doctors should do all right by him, he figured that much. The King's Horses hadn't been to university.

"I can help you if you are in pain," she said.

"I don't know," he said.

"I have medicine for pain," she said. "It'll make you feel better."

He felt better than he had for weeks. He lay in a freshly made bed. But he said, "Thank you ma'am."

The nurse injected him with medicine. At first, he didn't feel anything and then he realized he felt much better. He felt wonderful. He didn't feel like moving, but the pain in his body, he had not realized he felt, washed away. He glanced at the ceiling of the place, freshly painted crossbeams, a window that was open, and in the sliver there he could see out at the stars. He could see stars. He had not seen stars since he was working before he enlisted. Then he lay in a field with both hands behind his back; both eyes open in the darkness letting stars pass over him.

In this way, he passed many days. Occasionally, men in white clothes helped the invalids from their beds, and they moved around the room. It took several days for Martin to realize that he was not only injured, but that parts of his body were missing. They weren't broken. They simply were not there. He didn't have fingers on his left hand because the hand and the wrist, elbow, and arm it belonged to had been left behind. He didn't have an eye or part of his lower left mandible. It was gone, discarded on the field of battle.

His immediate thought on realizing this was to put it out of his mind. Don't think about it until he had to think about it. He could maybe go about his days with his face wrapped. What would his cousin think when he finally returned from the war? Would it be romantic to return wrapped like a mummy?

As he regained his strength, they moved him from the hanger filled with beds to a smaller place filled with other men like himself. They were missing parts of their bodies. Some men were just a head and torso attached to a body. They called them stumps. Some men didn't have any legs. They were halves. Some men had a single limb, a stray arm, a leg. They were worms. Among them, Martin felt oddly better. The misery of the stumps who sat at tables together, talking, or sometimes playing games with the help of orderlies made Martin feel like there was some hope for him. No matter how miserable, there was always someone worse off.

"What have we given and for what?" Martin wondered. He heard that they were winning the war and that it would only be a matter of time. But once won, would there be no more wars? That may be worth it. The death of so many men. The hospital filled with stumps, halves, and worms— this was worth it, he supposed, for no more war.

When he arrived they took him into a room and cut off his bandages. He didn't expect to see what he saw. He thought he would have a neat cut where his jaw and eye and ear no longer were, but he could see whatever had happened to him had not just removed parts of his bones and scoured his skin. He didn't have an ear. Most of his hair had not grown back where the skin had burnt. The majority of his head looked like a rump roast, livid, red. His nose curled, and flesh hung in sacks across the region where his eye had been. The marks continued down his neck, and the region where his shoulder and arm might be was now a smooth and burnished nub.

He began to cry. He didn't think of this being a possibility of the war—that he would be destroyed but he would remain alive. He was a twenty-year old man and had decades of life living as a freak, a monster, a living piece of battlefield junk. Up to this point, Martin had experienced no emotion except a sense of relief that he was no longer in the trench and that he had gone into the war and would be headed home when many people had not lived at all. He was not a stump or worm. But now he felt that there were worse things than death.

The aids removing the bandages didn't seem shocked by his condition. He looked at himself. One side of his body was untouched. He blinked. He moved his hand. His shoulder flexed. The other side didn't even have a shoulder. He blinked the tears from his eye. One of the aids looked at him. "You survived, mate," he said. "Fucking hell. You gave it to them."

"I am worse then dead," Martin said. "You'd shoot an animal that had this happen to him."

"You'll be surprised," the man said. "They'll fix you."

"How?"

"You'll get an arm, a tin nose, a glass eye. You'll look right again."

"How can I see out of a glass eye?" Martin asked.

"That'd be a miracle," the aid said. "Beyond the powers of science I'd think at this present time." He looked at the other aid. "But they are making improvements all of the time."

"I don't know," the second aid said. "Just the other day they worked out a way to rig up an arm where you can move the fingers with whatever is left of your old arm. I imagine one day they can attach a mechanical arm that can have a sense of touch."

"Before you know it," the first aid said, "They'll have an eye you can see out of. An eye like that can take advantage of progress. One day those mechanical eyes will be better than a real eye. You'll be able to see at night, and see through walls, see through girls' blouses. You'll be able to see whatever it is that you want to look at, and then people will want to put out their own eyes to get their hands on some mechanical eyes."

"You'll see," the second one said, not really realizing he was making a pun. Martin wanted to find a scalpel or something and cut his throat. He had made a mistake. Couldn't he just end this life and begin again? Next time around, no wars. He couldn't do that—not that he was worried about going to hell because he would already go there because of the men he had killed—but he couldn't kill himself because he couldn't do it.

The doctor came and examined him. "You're lucky to be alive," he said.

Martin didn't say anything.

"What would you like to look like?"

"I'd like to be as I was," Martin said.

"We can do that," the doctor said. "We'll have you fitted and sent back."

"Back to the front?"

"No. They won't take you back there. You deserve a nice holiday once you are patched up."

Martin wanted to believe this. He discovered there was a body shop they called the Tin Nose Shop. This was why they had sent him there to this hospital. An artist came. He worked from a photograph from Martin's enlistment. He drew a picture of what Martin might like once he was patched up. The artist wore a uniform. He carried the pad under one arm. He smelled of cigarette smoke and beer and was drunk when he sat in his chair to draw Martin.

Martin wanted to ask him if he shouldn't be drunk. This was serious business, but then Martin wondered how he would go about drawing a picture of whole people. What might the picture for a worm look like? The picture of a stump would be a fantasy. They could look like anything. There was so little of them left, they could be anything they like. I would like to be King George. I would like to be Harry Houdini. I would like to be Lillian Gish. It would drive him to drink, too.

He drew his picture and didn't even ask Martin for his input.

"Can I see it?"

"You can take a look," he said, "But I don't want to hear a peep. This isn't for a museum."

Martin looked at the image of himself, and it resembled him. He could tell the drawing was his picture. He had two eyes. He had both arms. There were things about his lost arm he didn't even know, though his lost arm was his. He never considered that he needed to record it so that it could be remade.

The nose was wrong. He thought he should say something. The nose is wrong, he should say. Had he not even looked at the photograph? A nose was a distinctive thing. "The nose—" Martin started to say.

"Not a peep, mate," the artist said. "Glad you like it."

"—is wrong."

But the artist had left.

A few days later they took him into the operating room and when they were done, they presented him with a mirror. They too had taken liberties with the artist's drawing. He tried to look around for it, but it wasn't there. He didn't resemble himself. He looked like a person, though. He was grateful for that. It was quibbling, really, to think that his glass eye color didn't match his normal eye. It was quibbling that the nose they had given him looked like the nose attached to a Greek statue and in no way resembled his original nose. He had a nose now, even if it was made out of tin and the flesh tone did not look like flesh. He cried again because he felt restored somehow, even if he was not put back to the way he had been. He had a piece of wood attached to his body that looked like an arm. He could fill out a suit.

He returned home on a transport and when he walked out onto the city street he was happy to be there. He carried his pack in his good hand. He went to see his cousin. He checked into a room. The woman there talked to him normally, and then suddenly she looked at him. She started to say something, and then checked him in.

He wanted to run into his cousin on the street. He wanted to see her, he did. He sat at a table at a teashop to wait. Finally, there she was running an errand to the store. There she was in the flesh he had been unable to draw, but knew as soon as he saw her. She stopped at the florist's. He went in to look at flowers. She glanced at him without stopping. She turned and asked her a question.

She had been in his mind's eye for so long. She didn't look anything like she had looked in his mind's eye. She was flesh, and real and her skin was skin.

She asked whether he'd come back from the war.

"I have, ma'am," he said. Did she not recognize him?

"Where were you? What unit were you in?"

He said his unit.

"That is my cousin's unit," she said. "Do you know him? Private Martin Bates. He was wounded at Ypres," she said. "He has blondish hair. He's about your height."

"I never met him," Martin said. "I'm glad to hear he survived."

As she looked at him, he saw she had not really looked closely at him, and then he could see that she could see that something was wrong with him. That there was something different about him. She still didn't see who he was.

"Oh," she said. She still didn't realize, he thought. Instead, she understood the lie of his tin nose. The lie of the dangling wooden arm. She didn't mention the lies. It was polite to pretend.

Martin bought flowers. "Here you are, ma'am," he said. He didn't look at her. "Thank you," she said. "Welcome home." She turned to leave with the flowers. He watched her as she left, careful to remember her features so he could draw them when he returned to his room.

The Simple Children's Home

I had known such things happened in the modern era, this is true. Fredrick's mother died in childbirth. There had been no warning that this would happen from our physician. Our physician wore a short mustache, drove a convertible, carried his implements in a stylish black box that seemed more like a lawyer's briefcase than the medicine bag still carried by the Bismark-era doctors who visited our elderly neighbors. Our physician was fluent in the latest advances in medical practice. When he discussed the advances in medical knowledge, he removed his spectacles and pinched the bridge of his nose. He said we had come far, and we had far to go, but each advance brought about remarkable discoveries. He proscribed a regime of vitamin tablets and mild exercise during my wife's pregnancy. She suffered from headaches, this is true, but she had always suffered from them. During her pregnancy with Fredrick, the headaches became longer but milder. She began to smile again. Flushed and glowing from her mild exertion after her walk we sat in the fading light of the day and thought about where we would move after Frederick was born. We would move to a house with a yard. I imagined walking toward the house with the electric lights burning and see her and our son in the window.

During her pregnancy, I worked in a factory where I checked drafts of technical illustrations in and out of the filing cabinets. One day I suppose I would have to begin to assist the illustrators. The efficient running of the archives was an essential function of the business. I preferred the work of organizing and overseeing the construction of the machines. We built printing presses. In the years after the Great War, all of Germany seemed to pay the price for our loss. Not only had a generation fallen on the fields, but there wasn't any paying work for the few of us who survived. I served at the very end of the war. I served long enough to know I would die, but even as I was training, the British discovered a mechanism for breaking the trenches. They drove armored cars through the trenches and once a hole had been broken the entire line dissolved. During those weeks of training it became certain we would lose. I returned to school and completed my training as an illustrator. I learned the habit of trimming my nails during my morning toilet because graphite would collect under my nails if they had any length at all.

When I found myself flush after working extra hours, I asked my wife to marry me. We married in the garden of the building. Her father and my father had both died during the war. At the wedding our mothers were there, still dressed in black. My mother already had a boyfriend, Oscar Funch, a man not much older than myself who worked for the National Socialists. No one really liked them, but they promised a future in a time when it seemed we had come to the end of things. Funch didn't seem sinister so much as someone who spent a great deal of his time figuring out who to cultivate and then cultivating them. Oscar Funch wore a plain suit and a beautiful white cotton shirt. He had a thick neck, wrinkled like an Alsatian. A scruff of white and gray hair covered his spherical scalp. He wore tiny round glasses that I couldn't see through from my side. They had the effect of blocking out his pupils. His eyes were two tiny silver discs. He paid no attention to me whatsoever, a compliment as far as I was concerned, because it meant he didn't regard me as anyone who was standing between him and his desired trajectory. His relationship with my mother puzzled me. I would ask my mother, but she was never someone who would talk directly to me. As a child, when I misbehaved, nothing would happen until my father punished me. I had trouble believing my mother loved Oscar Funch. He treated her well in the manner of the last century. He pulled chairs out for her. When she left the table, he stood. He fussed over her comfort. For a time, I thought it was an economical arrangement derived from their common cultural interests. They met at a drama club. They went to the theater, the cinema, and read the same books. Funch paid for dinner after my marriage. He grabbed me by the arm. "A glorious time is ahead of us," Oscar Funch said. "The old world has died, and a new one is about to be born. The progress of the race is assured." I thought this a funny thing for a man without children to say. He raised his glass. We raised them with him, and then he left us. We took the train later that day to Baden-Baden and returned a week later. I kept at my job and around me things did seem to become wonderful after the monotonous years following the war. Although there was a grinding energy, a forward movement that would eventually subsume everything, in those early years the changes seemed promising. New fruit appeared in the supermarket: bananas, pineapple, and mangos. New music appeared on the radio: swing, jazz. Cinemas began to appear throughout Munich.

During my wife's pregnancy, Funch visited the apartment looking for my mother. I was surprised to see him. I knew my mother had taken the train to Hamburg. From the nature of her plans, I had assumed she was traveling accompanied by someone, and I thought that her co-traveler could be no one other than Funch. I said she was in Hamburg visiting an old friend. Funch stood in the apartment. "I didn't know she was leaving," he said. "This is very surprising." Funch had up to this point been the picture of an urbane party functionary. That he displayed his anxiety so readily and openly surprised me. Whatever conflict had been between them, though, resolved itself so that the next time I visited them Funch had returned to his former unruffled self. My mother sat closer to him. She lay her hand on his shoulder at one point. Funch stood as if a massive weight had been placed on his shoulder, although her hand was tiny, a slip of pale skin and closely clipped nails.

A year later, my wife gave birth to Frederick. Despite our physician's mastery of the latest techniques, his precision tools, she died. The child we had named Fredrick was damaged in childbirth. At first, the damage wasn't apparent. For two years he was a joyful, spit-filled urchin who seemed like any other child. In this third year, though, he hardly spoke any words at all, despite spending his days with other babbling toddlers. I thought perhaps he was deaf. I took him to the physician to have him examined. The physician ran tests. I waited in the lobby reading about the advances in agriculture practices. We would soon be able to provide food to all of the people in the world using a combination of chemical fertilizer and efficient agriculture equipment. The doctor sat down while Fredrick happily played with blocks. "He isn't deaf."

"This is good news."

"He can hear very well."

"Excellent." I was happy to hear this.

"He is, however, simple. I doubt he will mentally develop beyond the age of three unless there is a breakthrough."

He didn't understand things; I thought me might be deaf. I would like to believe that I was shocked by the doctor's statement. A father knows his child. *Simple* seemed like Frederick. I had trouble imagining him as an adult. I wonder if this is how it is with all parents? Can they imagine their children grown? Or can they not imagine themselves the parents of grown children?

The doctor explained the nature of his condition. It may have resulted from the same cause that had killed his mother. They didn't understand the cause of the condition, but great scientific progress had been made in the years since the Great War. I could not help feel that there was a possibility that they would learn something. Many things that used to mean death had been identified as problems that could be solved. At the same time, I was satisfied. Frederick would remain mentally as he was—he may physically grow, but he would always remain my Frederick.

I contracted with a nanny during his young years. I played with him after work. Gradually it became clear to me that Frederick was a true imbecile. Frederick learned to speak but only with a great deal of effort, and even then he spoke baby talk well into his young years. I counted him as my only friend.

The National Socialists gradually assumed control. In Munich, the party had been active for many years. By the time they had gained control of all of Germany we knew that rather than merely control as an end, they had plans and control was the means. Even so, it only happened one step at a time. The only window I had into their extraordinary ascendancy came from Oscar Funch, who seemed to become physically larger each time I saw him. He sat on the couch to himself when I visited my mother. Funch held a saucer with his coffee cup. He smiled, and I couldn't see his pupils behind the tiny glasses like pennies on his eyes. My mother stood behind him and brushed his now mostly gray hair with her hands. She wore a beautiful dress, plain, black, and her blonde hair was pinned behind her head by a long silver pin decorated with pearls, a gift no doubt from Funch. My mother seemed younger than she had even when I was a child. She must have used a dye. She must have used a chemical to keep her skin so clear. She seemed natural and bright, though. She still kept up with the latest drama and film, but seemed less interested in it now. She said a golden age had passed, but that is the price, she supposed, for a strong government.

Germany was now at war again. The build up before the war had been good for my firm. We produced a great number of machines for the army. The war sent us into overtime. I couldn't see Frederick as much as I wished. He remained essentially as he had been at three years of age, even though he became older. I enjoyed my son's company. We played blocks and trains on the apartment floor during the dark winter nights. The gas fire emitted a great deal of heat, and we played until, sweating, we were driven into the kitchen for glasses of cold milk. It pained me a great deal when I worked overtime and asked the nanny to stay. She was a Polish woman, and I think she didn't understand Frederick. She told me that he was smarter than he seemed. It wasn't a matter of him being smart. He was as he was, and I enjoyed him for what he was since he wouldn't become anything else. I held out hope that he might have a normal life, but knew nothing else. The nanny seemed to indicate that Frederick was devious. He snuck cookies. She caught him one evening in the sugar jar. She seemed to think his attraction to these things indicated some kind of hidden cunning. I assured her they were merely an indication that all animals like sweet things. Frederick is incapable of seeing the future, much less making a plan, I said. Keep the sweets locked up.

After the invasion of France, I enlisted in the service. Everyone who could was expected to serve. I returned to the Army. It pained me to leave Frederick. I couldn't leave him with the nanny. I took him to a home for simple children. The facility was in Schwäbisch Gmünd, a distance from my apartment and the parks familiar to Frederick. But I would be in the war and they would understand how to care for him. The home was a progressive institution. When I took Frederick there he seemed unconcerned about the trip. He was excited by the novelty of the train. He kept making a chugging noise even when I told him to be silent. We passed the sweet shop, and normally I would scold him for begging to go in, but we went in, and I bought him an extravagant chocolate. It was incredibly expensive, and soon these things would become very rare, although I didn't know that then. He ate his chocolate and was content. He pointed out all of the things that were novel on the walk to the facility. For him, it was an adventure. It was only when they showed him his bed and locker that he began to understand that he would be sleeping there. He had bright red cheeks from the cold. A faint rim of chocolate coated the skin around his lips. He began to howl like a wolf. "Poppa, do not go."

"I must," I said.

"Poppa, do not," he said.

A nurse asked whether Frederick liked to play games. She had a canister of sticks. Frederick didn't have a game like this. It looked like the kind of game he could play. I was curious, but the doctor led me away. "What is that game?" I asked.

"Pick up sticks," the doctor said. "You drop the sticks and then try to remove them from the pile without disturbing the other ones."

"That sounds like a good game," I said.

The doctor stood with me for a second. "You can visit when you like," he said. "If you write him letters, we will read them to him."

"Thank you," I said.

"There have been many advances in treatment," the doctor said. "With the war, we will learn many new things. No one hopes for war, but after this war, the world may be a different place."

"Yes," I said. I had not been thinking about the war. If I died in the war, what would become of Frederick?

On the way to the station where I was to report, I stopped to visit my mother. Funch was there. He stood to warmly greet me. "You really look striking in uniform," he said. "Really very sharp."

Funch was as large as ever. He wore an immaculate, dark-blue suit with a tiny enamel pin with a swastika. My mother sat under him in a new blue dress; the blue had a rich azure glow. She seemed lost among the folds.

I was sent to the war and sent Frederick letters with no thought that he would send me letters in return, but he did. He sent me drawings at first and then began to write about his days in the home in thick careful letters. I had never thought him capable of forming a letter, and don't know whether they showed him how to draw them or if he had actually learned them. On furlough, I returned to the facility. Munich was very changed during the war. It was empty of people. The Nazis had removed the Jews to labor camps. I didn't know then the true purpose of those camps. I suppose I could have figured it out if I thought too much about it, but I was concerned with those things that directly affected me. Most of the young men were in the war that was now being fought in Africa and Russia. I visited Frederick in the home. He was well taken care of. But it was still a facility and I eagerly expected bringing him back to our apartment, to his own room, and playing railroad tracks with him again. In the facility, he lived in a room full of other children—some far worse off than he was—and I suspected that given the right environment and not great expectations he would live a happy life. That was all I could ask for my son. That is what I was fighting for wasn't it—a happy life for my child? I could fight for something like this.

On the way out, the doctor stopped me and told me some disturbing news. The Gestapo had taken some of the children. A week before my arrival they had inspected the house. They had a van and said they picked out some of the more severely handicapped children. "I don't know where or why they took them."

The doctor asked me whether I knew anyone I could talk to about it.

I did, I said. I knew someone. I thought about Frederick and wondered if I should just leave. But where would I go? The war might end, and then we would be exiles. I would be without work. This was the only life we knew.

I went to my mother's house. She had lost weight, and it didn't maker her look younger but rather had the opposite effect. Though her skin was even more amazingly smooth and ageless, even though her hair was a brilliant blonde, and her eyelashes were black and full, she appeared stretched thin. "I'm tired of this," she said. "Two wars in one life is too many." The war in the east was going very poorly that autumn. My unit was going to go. The thought was we had to win before the winter, but it was already early October.

I asked my mother if she could let me talk to Funch about the children missing from the home.

"Where do you think they took them?" she asked. "Men like that taking care of children like that? It is hard to imagine, don't you think."

Funch arrived. He opened the door. He wore a smart hat and hung it from the hook. He took off his greatcoat. He poured himself a drink. He assessed me. "The war seems to be treating you very well," he said. "You look very fit."

He poured a glass for my mother and for me. He handed me my glass. "I'm glad you included me in your visit," Funch said.

"I went to see my son," I said. I told him about the children taken from the home.

"I see," Funch said. "I also prize sentimental attachments."

"Can you help them?" I asked.

Funch looked at me. "Of course I can help them." He drank his drink. He said this not in a way that made me think he would help them. It was rather as I had asked him if he could lift a weight or drive a car. He had the capability.

"Will you help them?"

"I know who I could talk to. I question, however, if I should help them."

I looked at my mother. "What do you think mother, should Mr. Funch help your grandchild?"

She took a drink and looked out the window.

"Mother?"

"What difference does it make?" she asked. "We have all had a life. When we are gone, it will be as if we had never lived."

"I need to know whether Frederick and the other children shall be safe."

"I cannot protect them from the Russians," Funch asked. "But it won't come to that."

"From the Gestapo," I said. "The enemy wouldn't harm a house full of children. What am I fighting for if I am not fighting for the safety of my child?"

"You are fighting for the future," Funch said.

"What worth is the future if my child is murdered?"

"I will see that he is safe," Funch said. "I will look into what is appropriate." I had no idea what this meant.

"Mother," I said. "Don't you think your grandchild's safety is appropriate?"

"He is all we have," she said. "Funch, don't you see what my son is saying? Frederick may be an idiot, but of our prospects, he is all that is left of our blood."

Oscar Funch looked at her. His lips wrinkled a bit, I could not tell from disgust or mirth or something.

"I need your word that my child will be safe."

My mother seemed too tired. She seemed too thin. Her

clothes belonged to the body of a past body. I could see a gap in the back of her dress, a loose space between her skin and the fabric. "You will assure my grandchild is safe."

"Yes."

"I need your word, Oscar," she said.

"You have my word," he said. "I will make it happen."

I breathed out. "Thank you," I said. "Who wants another drink?"

When I left for Stalingrad, I was only worried about my survival. My son would survive, I thought, left in the hands of Oscar Funch. During that winter, I saw such things I do not want to describe. We had very little food. The enemy had even less. The war, such as I saw it, gave me very little hope that war would mean progress or even a future. We would destroy ourselves, which was perhaps not the worst thing.

When I returned to Schwäbisch Gmünd I found the house empty. The doors were unlocked. I walked through the empty building. The beds had been removed. The heat had been off long enough that icicles hung from the kitchen tap.

I asked an old man pottering in his garden in the house next door, "Where is the house?" The man wore gloves and carried a tiny spade.

"Relocated," he said. "The Gestapo came in vans and removed them. The doctor refused to turn them over. They shot him."

"They shot the doctor?"

"He should not have stood in front of the way of things."

On the way back to the train, I passed the sweet shop. It

was also empty. The bright awning had been removed. The building was filled with gray cement and trash.

I went to my mother's apartment. Bombs had blown apart much of Munich. She was as thin as ever, although she still retained the bright luster of whatever chemical she used to keep her skin in good order. She drank a cup of tea. "I'm glad to see you are well," I said.

"I am afraid I will wake up and not be here anymore," she said, "I keep losing weight no matter what I eat. I ate a chocolate cake until I was sick."

She didn't ask about Frederick.

"Can you arrange for me to talk to Funch?" I asked.

"He has had a promotion," she said. "He is in Berlin now. I do not see him anymore. I have not heard from him in two months."

"They relocated Frederick," I said. "I want to know where he is. Isn't there someone who can tell me where they were relocated?"

"What would that tell you?" my mother asked. "Why would you want to know a thing like that? He is in the past where we all belong."

The Ice Cream Man Cometh

I t was the summer I was laid off. "There is always unemployment," my wife said. "We won't need it, but there is always that." She pointed out that her brother, Able, lost his job all of the time. He always quickly found something. The only thing Able had was a chummy smile, and a dry, firm handshake. I had so many skills I couldn't fit them on a sheet of paper. In an interview my palm felt like a snail's belly.

My wife and I had moved into her old bedroom in her parents' house as my looking for work turned from a month into who knows how long. It still had the bluebell wallpaper she'd hung when she was sixteen. We paid so much in rent that getting rid of the payment along with my unemployment check almost put us ahead.

It was a tight fit for us. But it was nice to have Henri with her grandparents. There were babysitters in the house if we wanted to go out. We did once. I liked a place with a good beer on tap. There was a place, a faux-Brit pub called the Giants Causeway with decent local lagers on tap and Patsy Cline and Hank Williams in the jukebox. We sat in there and drank pints of cold beer. We said over and over, "This is nice," until we drank enough to believe it.

After several years of rain, the heat had come around. The spring had been wet then sunny then wet again. The weeds grew thick. In the heat, the wild grass turned yellow. Wild spores, ribbons of cotton from the trees, round wisps of fluff drifted across the yard. I interviewed for a dozen jobs before my last day at Safety International. They'd given me plenty of time. But, as soon as I had been laid off, a wooly apathy came over me. Why work? Even looking for work was as much work as work. I've heard it's a full-time job to find a job. Instead of looking for a job, I came home and nervously lay on the lawn with my three-year-old daughter. I felt guilty lying in the bright sun.

The ice cream man trolled the neighborhood looking for children. He played "Pop Goes the Weasel." The thin *tink atink tink* drew the children from the ramblers and split-levels. A mother in her busy-at-home sweatpants and track shoes escorted the children to the curb. She fished around in her purse for a few stray dollars. I didn't have stray bucks, track shoes, or even sweatpants. The truck drove by eight, ten times, a day. I kept the blinds drawn.

I moved inside to work steadily at the computer applying for jobs, researching companies, fiddling with the phrasing in my resume. I spent hours trying to recast the word "coordinate" into something with a punch.

My three-year-old daughter stopped in the hallway. "What's that?" she asked the first time she noticed the music. "Is that the music man?"

"Yes," I said. "He drives around playing music for the children." Looked at from a certain angle this was true. I couldn't very well have Henri fighting with me for ice cream every time the truck piped "Pop Goes the Weasel" down our street.

The ice cream the ice cream man sold never matched what I wanted when I listened to the cool, pinging tune. To say *The Music Man*, however, turned his stalking of my daughter's sweet tooth into a less invasive activity, into something in fact beneficial, a public service. She could enjoy the sound rather than crave the tiny little chemical licks he dispensed and that I could not afford.

Mr. Larsen, my father-in-law, had a spiral notebook of schedules for living in his house. Mr. Larsen had handled the notebook until the cardboard was as worn and fuzzy as an old dollar bill. The coffee pot always needed to have coffee in it. If you removed the last cup, you replaced the eight required cups to the line, marked with a red sharpie. He didn't want the machine plugged in. He wanted the coffee prepared using an exactly calibrated amount of grounds to water: three scoops to eight cups. The coffee had to be ground for twelve seconds in the Krups grinder. As the grinder sang and crashed, the operator had to rotate the base at a ten-degree angle to keep the sliced beans falling across the blade. It had been explained to me that a commercial grade grinder was really a mill and beans fell on a metal plate, and another metal plate crushed the beans. A domestic grinder actually *sliced* the beans rather than *crushed* them, and so technically these were coffee slices but not coffee grounds. A different thing, no? In order to ensure uniform slicing, ten degrees, slow rotation.

When Henri heard the music, she cupped her hand to her ear. "Listen," she said. "The music man!"

My brother-in-law, Able, arrived in his bright yellow Toyota Celica. He parked in the middle of the street and hopped out of the car. He wore white shorts and a white tennis shirt with stripes on the side that made his tanned skin as black as coffee beans. He bought an ice cream sandwich and handed the ice cream man, who I could see through the blinds was really a woman, some change. He hopped back in the car, gunned it into the driveway, and tapped the brakes. The car seemed to hop to its spot in the driveway.

When he walked into the house, Henri ran down the hallway to greet him. "Able!" And then she peeled, "Ice cream!"

"He's out—"

"No," I said.

"What?" he asked. "There is ice—"

"Shh," I said. "It's the *music man*. He drives around and plays music for the children. Isn't that nice of him?"

"You mean?"

"It's the music man!"

"That is cold."

"She'll figure it out one day. And then, our lives will be hell. Just give us one more summer of peace. Otherwise, she will wear me down. I can't afford it. She likes the music man. Imagine how much worse it will be if the eight or nine times she hears the music man, instead of the music man she hears the ice cream man and I have to tell her no?"

Able broke off a piece of his ice cream sandwich and gave it to Henri. Henri followed him into the living room. Able tossed the wrapper from his sandwich onto the table and set his ice-filled water bottle on the table. It would leave a ring. We were to keep the table clear of debris. Mr. Larsen said, "I don't want this table becoming a horizontal trash heap. Throw your junk mail in the recycling bin. Keep your bills on your desk. And, I must stress this," he said, "you must use a coaster from the coaster dispenser." There was a folk-style box affixed to the wall filled with cork coasters. A person removed them from the bottom and when they were done they placed them back at the top. It had flowers and a milkmaid painted on it. A picture of milk was in the center. Sometimes when Mr. Larsen sat at the table in the morning, he drank his glass of milk and contemplated the scene.

I was about to tell Able that his water bottle would leave a ring, but then he would say I was being the old man. I didn't want to be the old man. Maybe I would just hide when the old man returned, and then he could see that the rules that been broken had been broken by Able and I didn't have anything to do with it.

Henri played in her room. I trolled for jobs, wrote

applications, set an interview for the next day. I was busy working and Able was in the house doing whatever it was that Able did in the house. He had made the attempt to move out six months before to his best friend's house. The parents had retired and moved to Phoenix. Now Able and his buddy lived in the house. According to Able, having two guys in their early twenties living in a house in the middle of a suburb where they knew everyone was not exactly a good thing. It seemed like a good thing at first, but after six months Able didn't think he could take it anymore. Every night a party. A constant bacchanal, to hear Able tell it.

At four o'clock, the music man trolled through our neighborhood again. I heard Able in the hallway. Henri ran into the hallway, too. The three of us stood in the hallway listening to *Pop Goes the Weasel*. "The music man," Henri said. She cupped her hands to her ears.

"That is wrong, man," Able said. "That is just wrong."

He left for work.

Just after Able left, Mr. Larsen returned home. The car door groaned open, and then he pulled carefully into his spot in the garage. He entered the house, and I could hear him passing through the house on his inspection route. Henri came out of her playroom. The small TV in her room was on. She was watching her TeleTubby tape. She came out of her room and made her way down the hallway. "Grandpa!" she yelled. He laughed, and she laughed. He had some piece of chocolate for her or something because she squealed. Maybe Mr. Larsen was in a good mood today?

I came down the hallway then. They were in the living

room. Henri had a piece of red colored foil in her hands and was chewing. From the looks of what was smeared on her face, chocolate. Perhaps I would feel more amiable if he brought me home a piece of chocolate, too?

"How's the job hunt going?" Mr. Larsen asked me. This was pointed; I knew, because he tended to avoid these questions. Mr. Larsen himself had been out of work a few times in his life. He was no stranger to the lost weeks, the false leads, the confusing mess of trying to find gainful, even meaningful, employment. He didn't ask this question because the answer was never a good one. If there was good news, that I found a job, it's the first thing I'd say. I'd shout as he came out of the garage, "I found a job today!" Instead, I e-mailed three more resumes while he was making his inspection of the house.

"Nothing yet," I said. "As they say, finding work is a job onto itself."

"I couldn't help noticing," Mr. Larsen said, "that a few things were out of order." He took me through the scenes of Able's wreckage. He showed me the ring on the dining room table.

"A beverage ring," he said. "Left too long, the table will have to be refinished."

"Able came around today," I said. "I don't use this room because of the rules around this table. I eat standing up in the kitchen."

"Which leads us to the kitchen." He opened the coffee ground container. "This is empty." And then, he opened the coffee machine. "The old filter is still in here with the acidic grounds that will stain the plastic and leave a stale flavor in the coffee. This is one of the big downsides to a domestic coffee maker. I've been thinking about getting a coffee urn, just as they have in a dinner. This household drinks enough coffee it would be worth it. The coffee would always be piping hot. It would taste ideal."

He clucked as he removed the filter.

"These grounds are not uniform. To achieve uniform grounds, you must tilt the coffee machine at a ten-degree angle and rotate. Doesn't matter which direction, Northern Hemisphere or Southern Hemisphere, just turn and that will sort the grounds and achieve uniform granularity."

When we finished the tour of the house, I returned to the room to check if any of my resumes had generated interest, to escape the sense that I would remain here forever. I realized I would remain here forever unable to enjoy the company of my daughter. Instead, I felt compelled to spend the daylight hours feeding my resume to employer databases. My wife returned from her visit with her friends. Her keys jangled in the hallway and Henri ran to greet her and told her a story about the music man.

"The music man?"

"Pop!" Henri shouted and laughed.

Able decided he had to move out of his friend's house and get serious about his life. He came around in the truck to pick me up so we could move some of his bigger things. He was going to move back into his old bedroom. It would make the tight fit of my wife, Henri, and me in my wife's old bedroom even tighter.

The party house sat among other suburban ramblers in

a hollow surrounded by cottonwoods. The leaves in the cottonwoods muffled sound in the middle of the afternoon, and cast a dusky light over the eaves of the house. The house itself had seen better days. The lawn in front was worn where cars had parked on it. Trash collected in the ditch. Organic stains, tobacco, spit, spilled drinks spiked with bright, petrochemical dye faded in the sun-discolored driveway cement. The carport had been converted into an outdoor living room. A massive metal grill Able had bought at CostCo lay under a coating of grease and charred meat. A green couch lost its stuffing through cigarette burn holes. The matching green easy chairs sat in close proximity to the couch. The footrest on one had been ripped from the chair, leaving the long metal undercarriage to dangle. A stray metal piece stuck an arm toward the sky.

The house was locked, but the backdoor window had been smashed open, so Able leaned inside and unlatched it. He called into the house. "Hey!" The house itself was filthy but straightened up in the way that a thorough after-party cleaning left a house perhaps more picked up then it normally was—no clutter—but didn't address the underlying grit of the cigarette smoke, spilled beer, and the oily handprints on the walls. A barbell and a stack of 45-pound plates lay on the floor. The tip of the barbell had pierced the ceiling tiles, leaving them serrated. Between them, I could see cobwebs and yellow fiberglass insulation. The tip of the barbell had been wedged into a bundle of two-by-four beams. "We made a place where the girls could pole dance," Able said.

As we climbed the stairs, a woman with her blond

hair pulled into a ponytail and an oversized t-shirt and sweatpants and floral flip-flops moved out of the kitchen. She carried a coffee mug. "Hey, Able," she said.

"Is Tony here?" Able asked.

"He's sleeping," she said.

It was one o'clock in the afternoon. The carpets upstairs were destroyed. The edges of the carpets were in great shape, and I could see they were new, but the pressure of bodies and drippings in the middle of the hallways had fused the fiber of the carpet together. There wasn't any furniture in the house that I could see, except a massive TV set in the living room, and the remains of Able's furniture in his room, a huge futon, and a screen for his video projector.

"I have to get out of this house," Able said. "It was restored just before Tony moved in. Nothing to look at now."

We moved his things to his truck and then Able moved into his old room next to ours. I wondered, though, in moving why he would leave what seemed like freedom. Freedom might result in desolation, but if everything was already destroyed, what a relief, because there would be nothing to destroy. I could stop struggling against the fact of not finding work. I could sleep for an entire day. If I didn't feel like getting out of bed, I wouldn't get out of bed.

Able's occupation of the house immediately outmoded Mr. Larsen's rules. They became futile laws. As Mr. Larson's son, Able didn't do anything that was asked of him because he was asked to follow these rules a dozen times a day and instead he gradually ignored them and everything else that Mr. Larsen said. Able was seldom there anyway. He slept.

Around two he showered and then left the house, arrived just before his shift to change into black slacks and a white shirt and then he drove to the bar at the Marriott where he worked. Even though he was off by three in the morning, he usually didn't come back to the house until seven or eight in the morning.

He spent his afternoons, when the sky was bright, with friends on Lake Washington. His skin turned from a rich coffee and cream brown to a rusty black.

Buddies called for him during the day and I took down the messages, but no one seemed to know when Able would return.

When Mr. Larsen returned from work he wandered the house clutching his schedule.

My brother-in-law, like all of us, was no stranger to unemployment. Unlike me, though, he was no stranger to the pleasures of life. He always had a girlfriend, and sometimes he was on the phone with girls who were not his girlfriend either. My brother-in-law was at the house one day talking to my wife about what he needed to do to file for unemployment. My wife had never actually been unemployed. When she looked for work, she found it. Paperwork of any variety was her specialty in the family. Everyone had something they were good at in the family, whether they were good at it or not. Able was a handy man. In a weekend he fixed the bathroom, replaced the linoleum in the kitchen, and got to a half-dozen things that didn't seem that big of a deal when Mr. Larsen bought the place but suddenly become impossible for him once he was actually in the house. My specialty, I suppose, was in taking the blame.

After a morning of scouring municipal job boards, I sat on the grass with my daughter. Even though looking for work was a full-time job, at least I could telecommute. The ice cream man drove by—we could hear the van a long way off. Pop Goes the Weasel.

"Listen," Henri said to Able. She pointed to her ear. "It's the music man."

I just about jumped into the trees.

"You need to relax, dude. Come with me. We're going to go out onto the water. You're going to get drunk and sunburned. That'll set you right."

"Okay," I said.

"You've been cooped up at your computer since you lost your job."

"That's right."

"Isn't that the kind of work you did anyway? Being cooped up at your computer?"

"That's right," I said. "Employed or unemployed, I just sit at a computer desk typing away."

"Grab your trunks," he said. I didn't have swimming trunks, but I had a pair of khaki shorts, and I grabbed those. He drove with the windows down, and the air flowing into the car blew my hair around. A stray fast food bag in the back of his yellow Celica blew out onto the street. The air closer to the lake smelled like the water, the oil of speedboat fuel and the vegetable odor of milfoil. The boats made a whining noise from the shore. He drove along a wending road under a railroad trestle, past a lumberyard, and then parked in a bright field edged with poplars. I could see the field was really a makeshift parking lot formed by the sheer act of people parking there with their boat trailers. Able opened the trunk and from a cooler he pulled out two cold coffee drinks. We sat on a log under the shade of the poplars. Able's phone rang, and he checked the number and then put it back into his pocket. And then, he checked a message. "They are here," he said. We finished our coffee drinks and Able tossed them into the tall grass that had been the field before people started parking here. I went into the bushes and grabbed the bottles.

"What are you doing?"

"You're littering," I said.

I put the bottles on the car. Able tossed me the keys and then I put the empty bottles on my seat.

A gigantic black truck pulled into the lot pulling a bright red sliver of a boat. The truck turned around the lot and a woman who was as chemically conditioned as a Kraft caramel waved her hand with purple fingernails. They backed the truck to the boat launch, a crumbling cement ramp that disappeared into the sloshing black water. I hadn't noticed through the tall grass and reeds that there was a boat launch. Another woman jumped out of the passenger seat. She had hair cut very short to her head and wore cutoff blue jeans and quickly unsecured the boat and set it floating free in the water. In the water, it looked much larger. It had enough room for six people maybe to sit on their commute somewhere.

"Hey," Able said. He ran over to help secure the boat, and then the other woman came out onto the dock and climbed in. She turned on the motor. What sounded like a tiny buzz from the shore, in the fiberglass boat was a churning vibration that was more of a complete drowning out of all senses than a sound. Once the boat had backed away from the shore, it almost seemed to lift from the water. The hull sheared the tops of the waves off. The boat sped around a peninsula on Mercer Island and then veered across the lake into a bay near a park full of tall, scraggly pines. The sound of the boat sent crows flying. The bay was still in the shadow of the eastern shore. As soon as the boat stopped moving the water settled around us; tiny bugs flitted over the surface. Able threw an anchor over the boat and then pulled on it to check if it had caught.

"Not too deep here," he said.

"I'm Amy," said the girl with the caramel colored skin. "You're Able's brother-in-law?"

"I'm Ben," I said. I offered my hand.

She looked at it kind of funny and then gave it a powerful pump. She raised her eyebrows. "Pleased to meet you, Ben."

I offered my hand to the girl with short hair, and she just waved. "I'm Meagan," she said. "Nice to meet you." She bobbed her head up and down.

I wanted to say something more, but I didn't know women like this. The only time I'd ever come in close proximity to them was during Driver's Ed in High School. "Nice boat," I said.

"It kicks ass," she said.

Able had mixed Bloody Maries from some kind of chest in the middle of the boat and then we drank our Bloody

Marys and watched the insects dance in the water around us. It was very quiet, even though the far shore was full of houses. It was a workday, and everyone had already left for their jobs. The shore we were closest to was a park I'd been to before on land, but out in the water it made it seem as if we were in a stretch of wilderness. There weren't any other boats in the bay or as far as I could see. The sun broke through the branches and its light fell into the water, turning it from a dark opaque surface into nothing at all, just a clear transparent blueness streaked with long shafts of light.

Able dove into the water, and was gone and then he came up a ways from the boat and hollered, "It's cold."

I dove into the water.

Later, I asked what time it was. "I don't know," Able said. "I don't have my phone. It's in the boat"

We swam to shore and walked to a deli near the park. We were almost dry by the time we reached the counter. We sat on the green plastic furniture chained to a maple growing in the sidewalk planter. We ate fried chicken, French fries, drank bottles of cold beer. And then, we all walked back to the park and drank more beer while sitting on the beach. We said as few words as possible to each other. I asked the time again. Rather than remind me he didn't have the time, Able shrugged. We didn't say anything all afternoon. The four of us just nodded, pointed, shrugged. After a while the silence struck me that it was like spending an afternoon with cats.

Finally, as the shadows started to grow long, we swam through the cool water to the boat. I didn't get a cramp and drown despite swimming with a full stomach.

The boat started up again and then shot across the water. I didn't want to return home. On the way into the driveway, we passed the ice cream truck. And then getting out of the car the ice cream tuck passed down the street. Mr. Larsen wasn't home yet.

Henri greeted us at the door. "Did you hear?" she asked. "Did you hear the music man?" she asked.

"Yes," I said. "We should find the music man and see what he has for us."

We drove away from the house with the windows down listening for "Pop Goes The Weasel." It couldn't be far off.

The Vagabond

I n the middle of the night, nine p.m., while Morris was in the living room reading *The Systems Revolution* and drinking a glass of beer, and while Truman knit a sweater from yarn he'd salvaged at a yard sale and listened to the BBC news, someone knocked on the door. "Morris?" Morris didn't answer Truman. Morris didn't want to get the door. Truman asked, "Who do you think that is?" This meant Morris was supposed to get the door. A scraggly creature stood on the stoop. Her neck came out of her torso like a tree trunk listing on a muddy hillside. Her hair hung over her ravaged face. Something had flattened her nose. The skin looked as if it had been soaked in battery acid; it was mottled with pink and peach colors, pitted, and shaped like a crushed rubber duck. "Can I look in your garage?" she asked.

Morris had forgotten about the outhouse. He'd already replaced it in his mind with his planned remodel. The outhouse rotted under a thicket. Morris assumed the outhouse had fallen over, and the only reason it retained the appearance of an erect building was due to the abundance of weeds holding the walls. It hadn't collapsed, merely because it lacked the space to fall. Morris had put some things, for lack of anywhere else to put them, in there covered under a tarp. It was a dry, if musty, space.

"Tina and Tim's Love Wagon," she said. "We were T&T. That's dynamite."

"I'm sorry," Morris said. The poor woman was lost and didn't know where she was. "But it's late."

"There's no need to come out with me," she said. "I just want to look. I just want to see it. T&T, man."

"I'm terribly sorry," he said.

She blinked at him. She raised a hand. She had normal looking hands. Neatly cut nails, smooth white skin, with faint blue veins. She had pretty hands. She brushed her hair from her face. "No?"

"Goodnight," he said. He closed the door and then peeped out the peephole. She stood on the stoop for a full minute staring at the door. He thought she started to cry, but he couldn't tell looking through the tiny fisheye aperture. He wanted to open the door then and comfort her. Why not take her into the musty old place? There was nothing to steal. He didn't know her, though. He didn't know what designs she had. Truman and he had just moved in. It was still a strange place to them, and anyway, something about her bothered Morris.

Morris wanted that outhouse replaced with a new building of his own design. He wanted the roof shingled properly. He didn't care what was there before he was here. Now this was their house. He had consulted with some friends in real estate. They said it doesn't matter what is standing on a lot when you purchase a lot; you purchase the possibilities of the lot. This was a good lot, a double lot, a corner lot, a lot near shopping, near several parks, a lot, apparently at the source of the Piper's Creek. In buying the lot, Truman and Morris had bought their future.

And here was this person from who knows where? Who knows what she'd done to get to the state she was in?

Tina, if that was her name, moved down the steps and stood under the street light on the sidewalk and she started to walk around the house.

"What is going on out there?" Truman asked him.

"There is some woman looking to get into the outhouse."

Truman scuttled beside him, and they watched her walk around the house. She looked around and apparently didn't have very good eyesight because she couldn't see them standing in the living room window looking right at her. She crossed the yard and stood in front of the garage.

Morris rushed to the back door. He had truly lost his temper now. She wouldn't listen. "Goodnight!"

"I just want to look into the garage. Just a single minute."

"Have a good night," he said back into the house.

"Fuck you, mister," Tina said. She turned and walked down the sidewalk. Morris waited on the back porch, listening to the leaves rustle in the alder in the back lot until he was certain she was gone.

"Did she need help?" Truman asked.

"I'm very unsettled," Morris said.

"Let me make you a cup of green tea."

Morris worked the odd job as a systems consultant for Mr. Adams, who ran a number of startup businesses. Adams started them up and then Morris began to design the business. When they began to turn a profit, Adams' odd job accountant projected the numbers, and Adams sold them off. Every time Adams started a company, he received his new business cards, his letterhead, and his envelopes, he said, "This is it. I've found my line of work." Morris worked enough to cover the mortgage, take the odd class, and spend most of his time pulling knotweed and talking to the neighbors as they came home from work in the afternoon and took their dogs down to the park. Adams, each time his business turned a profit, called everyone together. "I can't stand this business," he said. He laid them off. In a few months, Morris got the call. Adams wanted to start something up.

Morris thought that he should find real work. But, he found something alluring about the repeated destruction of the company. He liked wiping everything out and starting over again.

Truman taught kindergarten. For him, each year was essentially the same thing: a batch of kids getting a little bit older. This June his first batch would graduate from the sixth grade.

Morris found out from his neighbors that the house had been occupied by a woman since the 1970s and maybe before. No one could say when she moved in. He didn't canvas the neighborhood. The topic just came up that spring as he worked in the yard behind the house. Thickets of knotweed, tiny alder trees, cattails, blackberries needed cutting down. The place itself: a single two bedroom house without a dining room even, pine floors stained with cigarette smoke that'd bled through the linoleum tile (that they'd removed), electrical wiring that was so old that it was just wires dangling by bobbins between the boards. All of the wire in the entire house had to be replaced. It wasn't designed to run the two computers, the fish tank pump, the assorted electrical contraptions required for modern life. The roof of the house had been newly shingled on the margins facing the street. Behind the house, the old shingles lay brown and cracked. From the street the house looked in good repair, and then climbing into the bushes behind the house, Morris could see another house, just about to fall down. But because of this, they were able to buy a house within the city. And although it needed to be repaired, in fact, *because* it needed to be replaced, Morris knew Truman would covet the house. Nothing pleased Truman more than to transform something old into something new. Morris liked the dual nature of the house. It was an old place; it was a new place. He drew plans while sitting in the kitchen. It was their house.

"What are you doing here?" Tina had climbed into the old outhouse despite his having asked her to leave the property immediately. "This is trespassing. I'm within my rights to call the authorities." She slept in an old paint splattered drop cloth that had been hanging from the rafters. She'd slept right on the black, packed earth. There were spiders and maybe even rats in there. Morris kept the lawn mower and gas tank against one wall. He checked the gas can cap to see whether she'd unfastened it to drink. It seemed all right. He'd heard of people so far gone that they would drink anything they could lay their hands on.

She stood up and blinked in the sunlight falling through the open door. He looked for the telltale signs of drug use, spray paint cans, crumpled bags, an ampoule, a syringe, something. He'd seen the movies. There didn't seem to be anything.

"Do you have everything that belongs to you?"

"Fuck dude, I don't know. I'm not even awake. I won't even know what time it is."

"It's time to go now."

"It was just last night. Did I even bother you?"

"I'd prefer you not sleep here."

"What are you doing with it?"

"It's not safe," Morris said.

Tina had her things, a backpack hastily packed and slung over her shoulder. She tucked her hair under a wool cap. She walked down the street toward the park. Cars rushed toward Greenwood Avenue where they worked their way to one of the freeways. They didn't even look at her as they careened past. Morris followed her down the block to the park. She crossed the field and lay on a bench in the shade. She stopped moving. He went back to the house.

Truman sat on the back porch in his bathrobe and house slippers with a muffin, jam, a cup of tea and the paper folded under one arm. "Good morning," he said. "Taking a walk?"

"That woman spent the night in the outhouse."

"That couldn't have been very comfortable for her."

"I ran her off."

"You ran her off our land? That's good. After all, you can't just have someone with nowhere to rest sleeping in our empty, falling down building. Better she find some overpass and sleep under that." Truman unfolded his paper and took a drink of his tea. "You weren't in great shakes when I found you."

"Thank you," Morris said. "I've said my thanks. I'll say thanks anytime you ask."

Truman didn't understand the implications. They had a house. It didn't mean that every vagrant on the loose at midnight could curl up in their outhouse. Morris went in and turned on his computer. He began his morning work redesigning a produce supply chain based on locally produced food. Before long he was only thinking in flowcharts.

At lunch, he went to the hardware store and bought a length of chain and a padlock and returned to the house and locked the garage door. He left the key in the key drawer by the fridge.

In the afternoon, Truman and he worked on the yard and he imagined what the place would look like once they fixed it all. And by dusk, he'd forgotten about Tina. He'd done a splendid job of putting her out of his mind. They ate their dinner outside under a string of lights. They brushed their teeth. They folded their covers under their chins.

Morris woke in the middle of the night. He drank a glass of water and looked out at the shadowy street. The dark lines of the power cables over the sidewalks moved back and forth in the wind. The alder tree rustled. It was going to rain. He wondered then what Tina would be doing out on a night like this? There were shelters. He didn't know. What would the harm be for her to stay in the shed? For how long though? It just wouldn't do. She would move in there. Or suppose she was a really good person to live there and gradually converted it into a kind of house? It would be very primitive, but better than wherever she was spending the night tonight, or she wouldn't want to spend any time there. People just a hundred years ago lived in worse places.

And then, he wondered if she was there now.

He set his glass on the counter and cracked open the back door so as not to wake Truman. He didn't want Truman's conscientiousness—his ready ability to sacrifice his own self-interest—to interfere. There was a lot of sound outside as the wind blew in the trees. The street light fell through the moving tree branches; everything was in motion outside. The padlock and chain were still in place. Through a crack, Morris peered, but it was too dark in the garage to tell whether anyone was in there. He tried to hear her. He said, "Get out if you are in here." He waited. He didn't want to say it too loud because Truman, that bleeding heart, would hear him and then they'd have to refloor the garage and move her in.

There wasn't a sound. Morris returned to the house and found the flashlight and the key from the drawer. Truman came out of the bedroom. "What's going on?"

"I thought I heard a noise. It's nothing."

Truman was drowsy and went back to bed.

Morris waited at the door until he was sure Truman had fallen asleep. The lock was still in place. He unfastened the chain and shined the flashlight in the garage. She was in the garage. She didn't move.

He called the police. He waited at the kitchen table.

"Come to bed," Truman called. "I can't sleep very well with you wandering the house."

"I can't sleep," Morris said.

"Drink some warm milk."

Morris wanted to go to sleep.

About half-an-hour later, he saw the cruiser. Morris hurried outside. The car stopped, and the officer stood in the middle of the street and shook his hand. They talked, and then he saw out of the corner of his eye as they went back to the garage, Truman looking out of the window. Truman wouldn't come outside, Morris knew, until he'd put on his pants and shirt. It was one thing to sit on the porch with tea and the paper and another thing to talk to the law in your bathrobe.

The officer shined his light into the back of the garage. Tina lay wrapped in the tarp. This time she had a bottle of wine near her. Morris checked the gas can. It looked as though she'd moved it. The officer shined the light in her eye, and she woke and stood up blinking. "Ma'am, can you please tell me your name?"

"Olmak Orrutundo. Some know me as Alice Hatchet," Tina said.

"Do you have any identification?"

"No, sir."

"This man says you are trespassing. Is that true?"

"Fine," she said. "Fine. He found me again. It's not like I was trying to hide back here. But, you all should know that this was my home before any of this existed."

She reached down for her bottle of wine.

"Are you going to take her away?" Morris asked.

"Do you want to press charges?"

"We do not want to press charges," Truman said. He was finally there.

"I don't want her to sleep in our garage," Morris said.

"Alice," the officer said. "You can't sleep in this garage."

"This is my home," she said.

"No, it isn't," Morris said. "Do you want to see the deed? Not a single one of her names is on it. She just showed up one day and asked to live in her garage. It isn't a fit place for a person to live. She needs to find a place to go."

"Where is that going to be?" Truman asked.

"Come on, Alice," the officer said. He took her into his car. "If you don't want people sleeping in your garage, it should be locked."

They drove away.

"You should just have let her sleep there."

"And then what? Build our new place for her?"

"She could stay there until we found her something to do. Once she got on her feet. I know it's not convenient, but it is the right thing to do."

"And in the meantime we have some hundred and fifty-pound simian living in our garage."

"She's a human being, not an animal."

"We are all animals," Morris almost screamed. "Where do you think she's going to shit?"

"I see," Truman said. "I understand why you're upset. We live together. She wouldn't live with us. She's just a guest. Yes, there are practical matters to consider. She could use our bathroom."

"Why don't we just give her a room? We only use the office for work. It would be more valuable, *in a human sense*, to let her sleep there."

"We have certain, essential obligations to others."

"Truman, where does it end?"

"I'm only talking about this woman who feels compelled to sleep in our garage. I'm not talking about all humanity. And besides that, it'll just give us more incentive to build the new place."

"That could take years."

"Not if she's there."

"She's crazy. Do you know that?"

"That is a stereotype. Not all homeless people are crazy. We all take risks when we allow new people into our lives."

"Olmak Orrutundo? Alice Hatchet? Alice Tina Whatever isn't in my life."

"We are all large enough to help someone," Truman said, "But she is gone. Never to return."

"Truman," Morris said, "I do not feel bad about that. Good riddance. I mean it."

The next day when she returned, Morris told Truman, "Alice Tina Whatever is yours. I'm going to the library." He rode his bicycle to the library and spent the afternoon reading *MMM: Mythic Modeling Modalities— Intraconscious Network Design for the Post-Information Age*, a book he'd read reviews of and because he hadn't even been able to understand the reviews he was eager to see the book itself. The book proved just as cryptic. He drank coffee at the espresso place. He didn't think about the lot, the woman, or Truman.

When he returned, Truman and the woman sat at the picnic table drinking iced tea. She had taken a shower. She wore a pair of Truman's old trunks and one of Morris' old oversized Oxford shirts. Morris realized he'd lost weight during his three years with Truman.

"There you are," Truman said. "You know Alice."

"How do you do?" Alice asked Morris.

"I am well thank you," he said.

"I'm Morris," he said.

"I know," she said. Her teeth were brown, and her skin was a little bit orange. She looked as if she'd been left to soak in leather tanning fluid for a long while. Even her hair held a kind of slightly brown, slightly off color.

"We got off on the wrong foot."

"I understand. I'm not too wild about you two guys living in my place either. But, what am I supposed to do? You own it or something." She laughed as if this were a joke. There was nothing Morris could hear in her inflection to indicate irony or even a sense of humor. The sound of the laugh itself sounded like the syllables mimicked by a myna bird. It was a noise that represented a laugh but wasn't actually a sense of humor expressing itself.

"We bought it," Truman said. "You know, Alice," he said. "You can't stay here forever. You will have to leave sometime."

"Where will I go?"

"I don't know," Truman said. "You can stay if you need a place to stay tonight or even tomorrow night. And as long as you do stay, we will need something in return for the inconvenience of having someone sleeping in our garage."

It became clear to Morris, then, what he was thinking.

"Today you have off. But tomorrow I want you to begin helping me pull up the knotweed."

She nodded her head.

"Understand, though, Morris doesn't want you here. And although I have compassion for your situation, I can't help but wonder how someone has become lost in the world. I may empathize with your situation and the things that have happened to you to bring you to the state where you need to sleep in our outhouse, but I can't support that kind of behavior. If we find you drunk, you will need to leave. Do you understand what I'm saying?"

She nodded her head and looked at Morris without any kind of muscle motion in her face. Morris couldn't tell what she was thinking. Maybe she wasn't thinking anything? He didn't know.

"The other condition is that if you stay here, I would

like you to consider what line of work you would find useful. I can help you in all kinds of ways. We live near thrift stores if you need an interview outfit. We can connect you with some social services, too. If you follow some basic rules, you'll be okay."

She started to cry. Or maybe she'd been crying, and Morris didn't notice until a marble-sized teardrop made its way through the cratered terrain of her nose and then launched into the air. And as soon as that happened, Morris felt horrible for calling the police.

With that Truman went inside to get dinner. Morris and Alice sat at the outdoor table unable to say anything to each other. She shifted in her seat. He shifted in his seat. He smacked his gums. Truman returned with rice pilaf and served it up on paper plates they had left over from the party, and they drank more iced tea and ate.

Alice told them about growing up in the neighborhood when it was still mostly farms. The entire world had changed so much since then, she said. "A woman like me could not exist then. I never saw a hobo or a bum growing up. They were all forced to live down where the stadium is now. And now we live wherever there is a place no one looks at."

"Alice, you aren't a bum," Truman said.

"Yes, I am," Alice said. "It means so much to me that you guys believe in me, but I am a hobo."

After dinner they sat in the living room. Morris read. Truman worked on his knitting. Alice sat at the outside table for a long while. "What do you think she's doing there?" Morris asked.

"Meditating," Truman said.

"I don't think so," Morris said.

"She's alone with her thoughts. It may not be as formal as meditation, but it is the same thing."

Finally, she went into the garage.

Later, Morris woke. It was dark. He sat up in bed. He couldn't relax. He'd been listening for her, he realized. He shook Truman.

"I'm sleeping."

"I can't relax in my own home."

"This is our home."

"We should have agreed on this before you invited some crazy person to live in the shack out back."

"She was going to keep returning. What would you do?"

"Just because you want to exploit some cheap labor, doesn't mean I want to put up with this."

"We'll talk about this in the morning," Truman said. "I'm sleeping now. I don't have a troubled conscious. But, while you are lying there stewing, consider the world from her point of view. It is our responsibility to help other people. Each individual action makes the world a better place. Think about that. Good night."

Morris waited for Truman to say something again, but he did just as he said, just as he always said, he went right to sleep.

Morris drifted to sleep and woke early in the morning with the thought that his dream house was on fire.

Truman and Alice began to work on the backyard, removing the knotweed. Morris worked in the office in the morning but found he kept listening to them. He could just hear their voices from the office. He wasn't getting any work done, so he took his computer to the library. At lunch he took his brown paper bag and sat on the library patio under the trees and then at the end of the day, he walked home.

Truman and Alice sat in the lawn chairs with glasses of iced tea and paper plates of rice and humus.

"Hey, look, daddy is home from the office," Alice said.

"How was your day at work, honey," Truman said.

"I have more work to do," Morris said. In the office, he put on his headphones. He found the loudest music he owned, a CD of Travis Tritt he bought in the last year of college when he tried and failed to learn a love of country music.

That evening, Truman said he'd learned a lot about Alice during the day.

"I don't want to hear about her."

"What's wrong?"

"Nothing is wrong. I will adjust to this new person in our family. But it will take some time."

The next day Morris worked at home. He took a break and watched them pull knotweed.

They spent the evening together on the lawn. Alice told them about the old neighborhood. She led them on a tour down to Puget Sound. As it started to become dusk, they arrived at the beach to see the sun falling behind the Olympic Mountains in the distance. The last of the light glanced on the waves and then the water turned dark. She told them how the park used to be busy in the summer with families from the farms around Piper's Creek. They walked back in the growing darkness. It seemed as if they'd come back to another time. They could see the old farms, the old neighborhood overlaid with the newer one and another one overlaying that. Each one lay over the other.

The next morning, Alice was gone. "See. The thought of her having an obligation to us, drove her away," Truman said.

Morris was relieved.

In the afternoon, though, she returned smelling like wine. A cloud of toxic odors, ammonia and methane, clung to her clothes. She lay in the tarp and slept.

Truman and Morris stood in the backyard. "What are you going to do about this?"

"I don't know," Truman said.

"You said you'd kick her out if this happened. You said you'd deal with this."

"We're responsible for her," Truman said. "She can sleep it off, and then we'll have a talk." Morris waited, but Alice never woke up. She slept and slept.

When they were going to bed, Truman went out and then back inside. "If she's like this tomorrow we'll have to go to the hospital."

"You said we'd kick her out," Morris said.

"Don't be cruel," Truman said.

It was too late, Morris realized. She had already moved into their lives. Truman had adopted her.

Morris woke late at night. He went outside. Alice lay on the lawn with the painting tarp over her.

Morris looked in the garage and checked the gas can. He checked the lid. It was still sealed. He undid the lid, and he could smell the fumes. He lifted it up. It was a good amount of weight in his hands. He looked at her sleeping in the lawn. She didn't even move. Although he had good reason not to, it wasn't reason that let him do it. He poured the gasoline out. He soaked the outhouse boards. The odor was now really strong. The can was light. He set it down and then found a piece of newspaper and wiped the handle. He checked his footprints. There weren't any, just the grass parted where he'd walked from the back stoop to the outhouse. He went back into the house and found the matches for the gas stove.

We can't help everyone, Morris thought. We are lucky if we can help ourselves. Truman lacked focus. He was never able to think about what was directly in front of him. For a time, Morris thought, he might.

Alice stirred in the grass, and he stopped. He stood in the door of the garage, struck a match, expecting the whole thing to burst into flames. It didn't. The match, in fact, fizzled and went out on the gasoline soaked boards. He took another one and flicked it and this one smoldered on the boards, and then a blue flame shot up over the timbers.

He went back into the house, sniffed his clothes, and they smelled like gas. He took them off and put them in the wash.

Truman was still asleep when he lay down. He lay still but didn't fall asleep. The light flickered outside. It sounded like something cracking, like something heavy getting broke. He imagined someone smashing something large and heavy like a sofa. Truman sat up. "What's that?"

Morris feigned sleep.

"Wake up."

Morris sat up.

"Something's wrong," Truman said. They opened their backdoor. Alice stood in front of the garage. "My stuff is in there. Everything I have."

"Have you been drinking?" Truman asked.

"What makes you think that?" Morris asked. "The wine bottle in her hand?"

"Call the fire department," Truman said. "Call the police."

Alice looked at him. "I didn't do this."

"You promised me you wouldn't drink if you were here."

"This was my home," she cried.

A siren could be heard now. The fire station wasn't too far away.

Alice turned and ran. Truman just waved his hand, more as if he were rubbing her out than a goodbye. "You can help all of the people some of the time, but you can't help all of the people all of the time," he said. Morris sprayed the wall of the house with the garden hose so that it wouldn't get damaged by the burning outhouse. In the morning, the outhouse would just be a concrete slab.

Tweak Tweak Little Star

Jules is in town for a week, and we're trying to make up for lost time. It doesn't start that way. Let me tell you how it starts. It's more like I haven't seen him in four years, and we have four years to make up in seven days, and so as soon as I pick him up at Newark things begin to slip beyond our responsibility. Helen doesn't want to come along to the airport. Did I point that out? Helen has sterling instincts. She's never been robbed or swindled or taken advantage of, really. She did marry me, but that's another story, so let's skip it. Her saying "okay, sure" to me guaranteed in my mind I'd left my young, wild days behind me back in Seattle. Jules sits in the passenger seat looking out at the Manhattan skyline saying, "I didn't know marsh and swamp, cattails and trees grew around the city. I sort of thought it had gigantic monster suburbs like right up to the edge of the city. But, it has cattails and big weeds and water and then the city rises up like a big ass ship right out of the waves." Jules has his legs folded under him, you know, sitting in what we called Indian-style in kindergarten. Jules sits there all limber. Just like that, I feel like a crusty old man.

Julian Peñor. That's his full name. Not just Jules. He's half-Filipino and half-Swedish. His mom is like an ice woman with her sharp angular nose and pointy chin. She once had long straight blonde hair that's white now, but was blonde when I first knew Jules. We often visited her in Ballard where she still lives with Jules' grandma, in an old Seattle home. We sat on her deck in the cedar tree shade drinking iced tea from chunky glasses. She showed us her tulips, thick fleshy purple and orange petals, fields of them growing out to the curb and down the parking strip, even crowding around the fire hydrant. Jules' dad, though, is Filipino and all of his younger brothers and sisters are full-blooded. They speak Tagalog in their house. His stepmother came from a wealthy Manila family. In Seattle, Jules says, she didn't have any friends because she wanted respect, first, for where she came from, and then respect for where she was now. Doesn't work like that in the States, Jules says. "Respect is the same thing as fear and she always thought it was the same thing as love." As soon as his dad retired, they sold the store and moved back to Manila. Jules says most of the time he doesn't think about his father or his mother's old house. He sort of grew up in the cracks between the old and new family. This is the same thing he used to say four years ago. Jules hasn't aged at all.

It's been longer than four years since I moved from Seattle. Three years before I came to New York, I lived in Idaho with my uncle. I could not hack Idaho. That was right after Jules and I got busted. They say it takes seven years for your body to replace all of the old cells. It's been seven years since that happened. I feel all my old, young, vital, and wild cells dropping off and getting replaced by these stuffy, old man cells. I'm going to be stuck with them until I'm thirty or so, and they're going to get replaced by even older, stuffier cells. Before I saw Jules, I was anxious about seeing him, you know, to see if he'd changed at all. But he hadn't. Talking to him I realize I hadn't changed much either, a few pounds here, some wrinkles there, the stray gray strand of hair I pull out, not that it makes a difference, but I've got to keep up appearances.

When he arrived, I immediately knew it'd take a lot longer than seven years apart before we wouldn't get in trouble as soon as we got together. It'd take until we got dead. Jules makes me feel that flowing, sparking, electrical current I haven't felt since I was seventeen. I want to show him a guaranteed good time, so on the way into the neighborhood, I stop off at the house of the guy who I buy my weed from and I get some weed and some meth, too. We aren't about to sleep if we have all of this city to see and seven years of lost life to resurrect and our old age to kill. We spend the afternoon hanging out looking at all kinds of places. Finally, we go back to my place.

Helen is just off work. She's in the kitchen drinking coffee. The light comes over the roofs, the fence, and into the kitchen for about a half-hour in the morning before we get a sort of early morning sunset, when the row of houses behind us cast their shadows over our back yard. Helen, as soon as she comes home from her shift, catches the light. It comes down, gets in her hair, and she smiles at us and says, "I've heard your name over and over again, Jules. It's good to finally meet you." She can smell the beer and the weed and because it's early in the morning, and we are as fresh as spring chickens, I know she knows about the crank. She nods and says, "Did you bring something home for me?"

"We are plumb out. We'll go get some more."

So the three of us are awake all of that day and until late the next night. Helen calls in sick for that night, and now she has two more days off, which is more time than she and I have spent together in a long time. Maybe a year? And we've got Jules with us. So, we don't know what to do with ourselves. Sleep is not one of those things that you want to do with yourself. Sleep is a necessary evil. It's as evil as death, which is also necessary although most people aren't going to admit that. We need people to die, or the entire world would be crammed with old geezers. As absolutely necessary as sleep is, people who get regular sleep are damned zombies in my book. They are the living dead, but then I know through hard-earned experience that a body must have some down time, because psychotic things begin to happen. My sweat has turned into cockroaches and if I have to have four or five hours of shuteye to keep that from happening, then so be it.

Jules and I catch up. His father has retired to the Philippines and that whole part of his life, the shop in Tacoma, is over. Jules says he never even goes to Tacoma anymore. Jules works as an office manager at Bank of America now. That's what he does. He says, "You know how it is, man. You say to most people, I'm a bank manager. Me. As if I'm that little thin name tag and title on my desk. Fuck my name tag, man."

Helen cooks a big dinner, and we play old records that Helen hates. Def Leppard. White Snake. The untouchable AC/DC. "Guys like you like rap. LL Cool J., stuff like that."

"No we don't," Jules says. We sing along to "Pour Some Sugar on Me."

We play cards, and finally Helen says, "I'm going to bed and leaving you two up to play and have a good time. Please turn the lights off when you go to sleep. Good night, honey."

Jules and I don't go to bed that night, either. We decide as soon as it gets daylight we're going to drive to Atlantic City and win a big roll and then retire to Mexico. I wake Helen in the middle of the night to tell her. She says, "Fine. Don't wake me up. I'm telling you right now, don't wake me up. I don't care what you do, as long as you don't wake me up."

"She thinks it's a fine idea," I say to Jules.

Later that night, I'm thinking about how much money we are going to need at Atlantic City. I don't have that kind of money, and Jules doesn't have that kind of money. I know that on one hand I'm beginning to tweak and should maybe lie down before all of the colors in the room start to get that sort of blanched look like a photograph that's been sitting under the rear windshield until the glossy coating on it has begun to peel. But instead, I say, "Let's go steal something." Way I look at it, I can sleep next week when I go back to work.

"Man, like what?" Jules asks. I can tell he's not sure if he likes the idea. But, part of him must like that idea because he doesn't flat out say no.

At three o'clock in the morning, we drive out into the Jersey suburbs, Patterson or somewhere like that, and it's just like it used to be between me and Jules. We drive down the block. He bends down in the grass, curls his fingers together. I take one two three steps and go right up onto the roof of an empty house, and slip into the open bathroom window. It's been a long time. We used to be pretty good about telling which houses are empty and which have people. We're not anymore, because this one has someone in it, some moron, some irate house owner with a Colt 45. He's an old guy, slow and maybe a touch of Alzheimer's. I feel sorry for him because I could see myself established and cozy, and I wouldn't want some young punk disturbing my sleep by coming into my house. But I'd have enough sense not to come at the punk with a gun. He says, "I've called the police." He steps toward me. The gun makes this click and then *blam,* a solid blow plugs the wall. The whole room flashes up, smells like cordite, and dogs start to bark up and down the street. I'm afraid Jules is going to take off and leave me stranded on foot. The house-owner turns purple around the edges of his cheeks and the tip

of his nose. I grab his hand, all brittle and the Colt feels
pretty heavy, the rubber grip still warm from the geezer's
fist. When he sees I've grabbed his gun, he freaks out and
starts begging me not to kill him. I have it in my hand, and
I place it up at him and he cowers down into the corner
of the bathroom, knocking over the trash basket, letting
out balled up Kleenexes. This is my fault. I came into his
house. I dive out the window with a grip on the gun. I'm
not even thinking about it. I jog out to the front where
Jules hasn't left, but has got the car revving up. We fishtail
on the loose suburban gravel shoulder, and then catch the
pavement and take off.

"That's a nice gun," Jules said. "It's a loud gun."

I look at the Colt 45 for the first time and realize I
still have it. "He shot at me." Jules and I laugh and keep
driving. I put the gun under the seat.

When we get home, we shoot some speed, and cook
breakfast, even though we don't feel hungry, but we know
we have to feed our bodies and Helen will be hungry when
she wakes up. We shower and after I've dried off and have
a cup of coffee and I'm sitting in the kitchen with Helen
and Jules, and the whole memory of what happened has
faded, I think that's all right, what do you expect me and
Jules to do when we get together in New York City? Get
fucking in trouble, that's what. And I feel ecstatically at
peace and happy and whole and young. We are going to
Atlantic City.

We can't smoke in the car because it makes Helen sick.
Smells make Helen sick. She carries a vial of vanilla oil
with us as we walk through Manhattan, stopping to sniff

it. I didn't realized the smell of that place, greasy clouds of cooked cheese, tomato sauce, and festering garbage heaps. She tells me ladies in the old days used to carry nosegays to keep the smell of the city out of their noses.

We start drinking on the way out of New York. Jim Beam, just a shot for the road and then we run into a long line of traffic and I have some more and Jules has some more.

I'd packed for the trip to the Atlantic, a picnic blanket, the sand toys, bucket and spade and mold for the castle towers all bright blue plastic.

Helen says, "Maybe I should drive and you two should take a nap in the back seat? You aren't making any sense."

I say, "We are as right as rain."

At a Service Area on the New Jersey Turnpike, somewhere south of Fort Dix, a man starts talking to us. I open my door. I stumble when I open the door. Every time I get out of the car, my foot catches on the seat belt and my arm on the steering wheel. I untangle myself and just as I stand, before I can see what kind of general fool I've made of myself in the public of the Service Area, this man starts talking to me. "... my wife and two kids are in my BMW a couple of miles down the road, and my credit card isn't working for some reason. I'm an engineer, and I live in Scaggsville and I just need a hose for my car. It costs 42 dollars, and I just have twenty dollars." Standing there, I keep thinking, doesn't your BMW come with a service plan?

I'm flummoxed and don't know how to say fuck off to this loser because I sympathize with him if this is a real situation, because if this is how he thinks he's going to get out of it, he's an idiot. Before I even completed that thought, I'm on to what in the hell, is this a scam because this is a stupid really obvious type of scam. I might've tried to pull something similar if I've ever been in the business of cons, but this is really incompetent as scams go. Jules and I would just take their money. This guy's maybe around our age, so he's old enough to have added some polish to his routine unless he's new at all of this. I can't just give him money, although the detail keeps coming and it seems very real, this man's problem, but I can't just give money to any bum on the Turnpike who needs help. Doesn't he have anyone to call? He prevails on Helen and Jules and me because we look like people who can help out someone in desperate straits.

My wife steps out of the car wearing her yellow dress and white flats. Her hair is stiff. She has a wicker purse that looks pretty nice, all told, with her sunny beach attire.

I am about to ask this guy about his service plan and even offer to give him a ride back to his nonexistent car when my wife cuts him off. I want to rub his nose in his stupidity, the plan, his way of life, how he should see it isn't free. He is probably thinking first of all that he can get away with it and second of all that really it doesn't hurt anyone. He depends on people being suckers, and nobody likes being a sucker because then they've been had. Given the choice of being robbed or suckered, I'd say ten out of ten would rather be robbed than suckered, I mean given the choice.

"Sorry," Helen says. "But we have just enough money

to get us through the tolls." This was valid. Sure we could get some more money, but her statement was true. The man shook his head and said thanks and then wandered off to ask someone else for help.

"Thanks," I said to Helen because he is gone. I stand there imagining giving him a ride down the road, and then he produces a handgun and asks us to pull over to the side of the road, turn on our hazards, and then leads us out into the field, where he shoots me and my friend in the head and then rapes my wife and then shoots her in the skull. Or, he shoots her in the head and then rapes me and my friend and then shoots us in the skull, depending on his mood, and the moon, and so forth. The weather is a powerful motivator.

We walk into the service area. A heavy woman stands in front of the cash register. Another woman pushes a pallet full of boxes, frozen hamburgers, boxes of soft drink cups, to the burger stand. The woman behind the cash register turns to the heavy woman and asks her, "What do you want?"

"I want some change. I need some change. I'm out. Barney fucked me with the change again."

"Here you go," she says and hands her a fistful of change and takes her five-dollar bill. I order coffee. It comes in a thin Styrofoam, blue cup. I drink it while I walk around the tiled space under the skylights. A ring of vending machines circles the skylights and visitors' guides to Pennsylvania and New Jersey. While drinking my coffee, I walk outside where it's cooler. I look for the man. I can't see him.

I walk back to the car and check the locks. I lean down

to each handle and jiggle it. The lamppost nearest the car jostles in the wind. It shuts off, and then the wind knocks it another way and it turns on. When it's dark, I can barely see the cars parked at its base and then it flicks on and everything is too bright and I can barely see the cars at the base. I walk back to the Service Area and stand near the bushes and watch the cars pulling off the turnpike, the people getting out of the cars and stretching and then going into the building. The man comes down from the gas station and stands where any car would have to pass him. Several cars pass him, and no one stops and no one gives him any money, thus voting, as I pointed out, ten for ten would rather be robbed.

We watch the guy walk around under the stark lamp light, and then the wind shifts and it goes out.

"Come on, lets go," Helen says.

I want to catch this guy lying. I want to force him to admit that he is trying to get people to hand over their money. I say to him, "We can go pick up the cable and give you a ride to your car." I want to prove to him that my life is better than his life.

Helen says, "What?"

"It's all right. I want to help someone who is on the road and needs some help," I say.

"Can I talk to you, honey?"

"Sure."

"In private?"

"Excuse me," I say and roll up the window.

"Look, this man needs help, right?"

"This man is scamming us. There isn't a car. What are

you going to do with him once you find out he's lying?"

"Maybe he'll move on," I say.

"He can move on right now."

"I want to see if he's lying." I roll down the window. "Well, what about it?" I say to the man.

The man says that he doesn't want to put us out. "It's alright," he says. "I don't want to cause any trouble. It would probably be easier for you if you just gave me the money, and I walked over to the auto supply and back to the car."

"If you have your woman and your kids in the car," I say, "then it wouldn't be safer. You don't know what kind of people you are liable to meet on the road. Someone could come along and rape your wife and kill your kids or kill your wife and rape your kids, or hell they could rape and kill and mutilate everyone."

"If you don't mind, I don't want to make any more trouble than I've already made."

"Are you afraid to get in the car with us?" I ask. "*We* aren't going to hurt *you*."

He gets in the car, and I start it up. Helen and Jules don't say anything. Jules sits next to the man and nods at him. "How you doing?"

"Everyone buckled up?" I ask. "Remember, It's not only common sense but it's the law."

"You said you were an engineer?" Jules asks.

The man nods and looks out the window. He looks around the car, at me trying not to tweak out in the front seat, at Helen holding her fingers across her eyes, at Jules smiling at me in the rearview mirror because he can't wait for things to turn out however they are going to turn out.

"What do you work on?"

"I design refrigerator parts," he says. "I work on handles mostly, stress analysis, things like that."

I ask him, "Where is this auto supply place you're talking about?"

"It's in Harris," he says.

The only way I can get off the Turnpike is to drive down for about ten miles. If his car is where he says it is, I'll pass it. "Should we stop and see how your kids are doing?"

I say, "How about I drive down and then drop my friend and wife at your car and then we can go pick up this part in Harris? That'd be a long walk, you know?"

Helen has the map out and says, "Yeah, it would be thirteen miles."

"I was planning on hitching a ride."

"Then we're doing you the right kind of favor, ain't we?" I say.

"Thanks a lot," he says.

We ride on the Turnpike. The car picks up speed to about sixty-five miles an hour. After about thirty seconds of driving, the windows start to cloud, so I turn on the defrost. After about three minutes, Jules asks the engineer if he'd like a drink. My friend pulls the bottle of Jim Beam, now about half-drunk, from under the seat.

The engineer says, "No thank you."

Jules pours a shot into the Styrofoam blue Maxwell house cup he drank his coffee out of. The sweet cleaning fluid smell of the whiskey fills the car. My friend drinks the shot and then smiles into the rearview mirror.

"Would you like some?" Jules asks me.

"Don't mind if I do."

"You're driving," the engineer says.

"An acute ability to observe the obvious," I say. "That's what makes for good science. The scientific method is mankind's greatest invention. As an engineer you would agree to that. I don't think I caught your name?"

"Larry Carson."

"Nice to meet you, Larry. My name is Cosmo Kramer. This is Elaine Bennis. George Costanza in the back seat."

"How do you do?" Jules says. "Sure you don't want a snort?"

Larry Carson took a drink.

"You sure walked a long way," I say.

"I did," Larry says. "I sure did. I think you are just about there, though."

It's dusk and foggy and cool outside. It's late winter or early spring, that middle line between the two where it could rain or snow or get sunny and warm, either way. We pass an occasional cherry tree, an explosion of white blossoms turning a little brown. Otherwise, the sides of the turnpike are just scrub pine. Along the side of the road a dirt road comes down close to the shoulder.

"I parked down on that road," Larry says. "The signs say don't park on the shoulder. So I didn't."

I slow down and then drive the car bumping and jostling over the shoulder, the gravel, the margin of grass, onto the bushes. The car pops onto the road.. Helen hisses. "What in the hell are you doing?"

When we are on the dirt road, I stop the car.

"Which way?"

"What?" Larry says.

"Which way did you go?"

"That way." He points down the road. "I can get out here." He starts to open the door, but I step on the gas. I drive along at about twenty miles an hour. The thick grass growing up between the ruts rustles on the car hood, leaving behind stray seedpods. The road turns into the pines. We can see the Turnpike and the cars on it, and then Larry says, "Stop the car."

I stop the car and reach under the seat.

"What are you doing?" Helen asks me. "Let him go."

Larry tries to unlock the door, and then he bangs the heel of his hand against the glass. "Can I get out?" he asks politely even though he's banging the door. I unlock the door and turn around with the geezer's Colt in my hand. "Larry," I say.

"Where did you get that gun?" Helen asks. "It doesn't look cheap."

Larry has the door open and then tries to get out, but he still has his seat belt on. He reaches down and unbuckles it, trips, and falls out. He does all of this without even looking at me. I open the door and stand on the soft, loamy soil under the pines.

"Larry," I say.

Larry stands away from the car. I can't really see his face in the dusk. The light from inside the car covers his body, but doesn't show his face.

Larry backs away from the car.

"Larry, you were lying about your family, weren't you?"

"What do you want?"

"Just tell me the truth."

Larry jumps into the pine copse. I fire. Helen screams. I roll away from the car, and run into the woods after Larry.

Well, I don't run, not sprinting. I jog. I think, then, I did hit him. Right in the darkness beyond the road, where a little light comes down through the opening where the road runs, it's sort of dark. Larry lays in the pine needles still breathing. He holds his stomach, covering a growing splotch on his sensible sweatshirt. His eyes are all buggy. He looks at me, and I look at him.

"What's your real name?" he asks.

"Sometimes people get into trouble when they are traveling in strange places," I say. "Sometimes they need the goodwill of strangers. People like you make it hard for them."

Larry rolls his eyes, and stands up which must be a gigantic effort considering what has happened to him.

I don't feel real remorse at that second shot, not real remorse like I did when I was a kid and shooting starlings, the only bird I was allowed to kill. I could collect piles of them. My father paid me a dime for each one and I felt a little shame each time I leaned into my twenty-two and fired, and one of them fluttered to the ground. Now, I feel like, Well shit, I'm committed to this. I think, originally, I wanted to scare him, this con man who basically was holding up decent people and turning cynicism loose on the earth and now I have to get away with it. I shoot him and if I don't kill him and bury him, he'll turn up.

I look around at the pine trees. I pop him in the skull.

He falls into the soft soil. I walk back to the car.

"What happened?" Helen asks.

"I don't want to talk about it. I need a drink."

I put the gun under the seat and pop the trunk and then go back to the trunk. I look at the crowbar, the jack, the picnic basket we are going to use when we get to Atlantic City, and the plastic bucket and spade we're going to build sandcastles with. I take the bucket and the spade.

"I need to bury him," I say.

"Did you kill him?" My wife asks.

Jules, who'd been around with me long enough to know shit happened, just looked out into the darkness. "I'm not going to help you with this. I should by all rights tell the cops, but I'm not going to; I am not going to help you though, I'm just going to sit here with Helen and wait. Shit man."

My wife looks at me standing in the pines outside the car. "You killed him?"

"I didn't mean for anything to happen. I was trying to scare him. He shouldn't have ran."

"You shouldn't have picked him up."

"He was asking for trouble."

"He wasn't asking to be killed. Even if he was asking to be killed, you shouldn't have killed him. People do not have this conversation." Helen reaches over and turns the lights off. "I don't want the batteries to run dry while we wait for you."

"Have you ever dug a grave before?" Jules asks.

"Fuck no, I've never dug a grave before. Is that something they teach bank managers now?"

"Oh shit," Jules says, "This is some trip to Atlantic City. Big Winner."

We walk into the pine trees and find a small clearing. I begin to dig.

Jules drags Larry to the clearing and then checks the guy's pockets. He has twenty-three twenty-dollar bills. "Jackpot," Jules says.

I take off my shirt and pants. I fold them up. The ground is cold.

I use the spade to break the earth. The little plastic shovel bends and won't break the soil. It's only a toy, and I shouldn't get mad. I cup my hand into the sand, getting grit stuck under my fingernails. Once I have about six inches dug in a trough maybe two feet wide and five feet long, I use the plastic bucket. I scoop the soft soil out, and the soil all holds together like a little tower. With each scoop, I lay down another tower until I have this big mound of towers.

"Where most people make the mistake," Jules says, "is that they dig the grave too shallow. You need to make it six feet deep. You also need to heap up soil in a mound so that as the body decomposes it doesn't leave a depression. They look for depressions."

"How do you know this?"

"Shit, I don't know. I got morbid interests."

"How likely do you think it'll be that I'll get caught?"

"Unlikely, as long as they don't find the body. You see this is a random act. There isn't anything to trace you to the body. It's also unlikely anyone will report this guy missing. It's like he's missing already."

I keep digging. Jules smokes and walks back to the car

and checks on Helen and then comes back. "She's asleep," he says. "I can't believe that."

The exertion of digging the soil out of the grave covers my body with sweat and little bits of gritty sand. Finally, I have a heap of soil. Standing on my tiptoes, I can look out of the grave. "Hand up?"

Jules leans down and hauls me up. I drop the body into the grave. Larry rolls into the hole about halfway down to a shelf I left because I wanted to speed up the time it was taking me to dig this thing. "Man," I say. I lean down and shove him down into the grave. The sole of my foot rests on his cool skin. It is like standing on damp linoleum. I scoop the earth back into the grave. There is just a heap. I put back on my clothes and go back to the car. We sit there and drink the rest of the bottle of Jim Beam, and then I walk back to check everything out, just to make sure I didn't leave anything. I forgot the plastic bucket, and that's it. It's very late now. There aren't any other cars on the road. In Harris, I stop and Jules and I rent a room. I shower and put on fresh clothes and then we continue driving. At dawn, we come to Atlantic City. Helen stirs and then looks at me driving and then at Jules snoozing in the back seat.

"Did we pick someone up?" she asks.

"We did," I say. "That guy who was asking us for money."

"What happened?"

"His wife had a cell phone and called a tow truck. If we hadn't given him a ride back, she'd have been long gone."

"I don't remember that."

"What do you remember?" I ask.

"Did we park under the pines?"

"That's where the BMW and tow truck was."

"I guess," she says. "I had this dream that you did this crazy thing. You shot the guy."

"Why would I kill someone?"

"You do crazy stuff sometimes. It seemed so real."

"What seems real about me killing someone? Don't you remember the tow truck driver talking to us? Big guy with a beard and overalls?"

"I guess," Helen says. "I guess I remember that. She looked out the window. "Atlantic City!"

"Wake up," I say to Jules. "Wake up, we're in Atlantic City."

He wakes up and smiles and reaches under the seat. The bottle of Jim Beam is empty.

"I'll have to fill you in on what happened."

"I don't care what happened," Jules said. "We're in Atlantic City, and I need a drink."

The Penile Colony

My first father worked as a mechanic on airplanes, but he couldn't fix his own car, a 1939 Pontiac with secondhand wheels with wooden spokes. It had wheels like a Conestoga. He enforced his rules with a swift smack to my back. My second father worked in a bank and came home after six tired. He took off his jacket and lay on the couch where he snoozed until dinner. After dinner he had a glass of sweet wine that was as thick as molasses and the color of cola. That improved his mood for about half an hour so I could stand him. We played a game of chess. He always won, except for our last game. I started to study chess books and learned chess traps. We sat down to play, and within ten minutes I had him.

"Checkmate," I said. "Checkmate?" He repeated back to me. He sat looking at the board for a long time. "Well," he finally said. "That settles that." We didn't play chess anymore. He never told me his rules, but I knew them.

My third father designed control panels for submarines. He talked with a slow, country drawl and always wore a felt hat. When it rained, which it always did in those days, the hat turned funny colors and all splotchy like a giraffe's neck. He used to tickle me until the insides of my rib cage felt bruised. The muscles in my belly twitched. He hooked a finger, when I was paralyzed with laughter, under my bra, and peeled it back so that the cups squashed my boobs. He acted like he didn't know what he was doing. When I squirmed away from him, he would walk slowly after me calling out in his country drawl. During his regime, I lived through an uneasy lawlessness.

After Mom married my fifth father, I asked her," Why do you marry every other man you meet?" It was getting so that every loony psychopath and social misfit got wind of her divorce and lined up. "I am in love," she said. This was her answer for everything. When she started to get ready to kick me out, she told me she loved me. Love for her was the beginning and the end of the story. I figured by my fifth Dad that for Mom it was easier to find a man than find a job. This father came with his own set of rules he wrote on an old piece of cardboard he secretly nailed to the back of the garage door where I wouldn't see it until I broke one.

After Thanksgiving in the early days of the 1960 Christmas shopping season, when the stores were just getting decorated, and the Salvation Army Santas had just set up buckets on the sidewalks, Mom kicked me out of the house. She said if I wouldn't follow the rules of the house, I could figure out how they worked on the street. She might have thought that after a few days I would return home contrary and eager to do as I was told. Problem was, I was always eager to do as I was told. I just had trouble figuring it out.

I took my bag and went downtown and rented a locker at the Greyhound bus station. When sleep arrived, it didn't matter that my body wasn't lying in perfect repose in freshly laundered sheets with soft pillows. I slept most of my life in sheets on a mattress in a room with a door and the familiar shadows of stuffed animals, my chest of drawers, the faint odor of my mother's dinner lingering in the house. She boiled meat. On the huge wooden benches at the bus station, I approximated sitting, lolling until my head curled into the embrace of the wood worn by the scalps of countless passengers waiting for their cross-country buses. At home, sleep rolled out through the night and I would reluctantly wake in the sheets staring at the morning light streaked across the ceiling of my room.

In the bus station, I woke throughout the night to check the area around me to make sure some pervert, or drunken sailor, hadn't sidled up to me. My neck kinked as I came to at some early morning of the hour to find a sailor in his whites sitting a respectable distance on the bench next to me. He had his hat over his privates, and the hat danced up and down. I stood suddenly, pain flaring in my back, in my sleeping legs, and I grabbed my coat. I staggered into the middle of the bus station. No one else was awake at that hour. The sailor watched me move. He wasn't an ugly man, or even plain, but somewhat handsome. His face was flushed from whatever he had been doing to himself. He adjusted himself. He had bothered me, but at least I figured the sailor was honest about what he needed and how he would get it. He was actually looking at me, but, once I was awake, he swept himself up, leaned on the bench for support, and disappeared out the door into the cool middle of the night. I was awake but aware of the fuzzy feeling in my neck and the back of my knees. I still needed sleep for school in a few hours. I returned to my spot and returned to my troubled slumber. I adjusted myself when the pain of sleeping in an unnatural position became too much.

I showered at the YMCA and then caught the bus to school. In the evening, I returned to Seattle. I sometimes stayed at school for as long as possible because I didn't have anything to do. I hung out in the art room and drew pictures. The art teacher and sometimes my English teacher drank coffee together and commented on my drawings. I listened carefully in order to follow their instructions. My English teacher said his wife was an artist. At four o'clock, I bought a cup of soup at the dinner and drink a cup of coffee and did my homework, and then finally I napped on the bus.

After two weeks, I let it drop I was sleeping in the bus depot, and one of my friends offered for me to stay at her house. When I moved in, it became clear she wanted company in everything she did. She wanted me to follow her around. If she was reading a book, she wanted me to turn the pages. One night I told her I would have some coffee with some friends. She got her coat. "I'm going by myself," I said.

"You mean without me?" she asked.

"I'll be back," I said.

"You mean I am not invited?"

"I just need some time alone," I said.

"You mean away from me?"

"We can have coffee together tomorrow night," I said. In the morning, she wouldn't talk to me. I didn't want to go back to her house after school. I did my routine of going to the art room and drawing and killing time. Finally, I went back to her house. It was a week until Christmas. It was raining. They had a Christmas tree. Her parents sat under quilts in the living room watching a program and drinking hot chocolate. "Hey Marge," they said. My friend kicked me out. She had packed my bag. "It was getting old anyway," she said.

I ended up at my English teacher's house in a deal where I would watch their kid, so he and his wife could live an approximation of their life before they had a kid. They were beatniks. Jim had a tiny little patch of beard on his chin. Eva wore stripped t-shirts and cardigans. They both read books and listened to jazz. Their house was small but lined with shelves. I had a room in the basement next to the laundry room. The other room had a cement floor and was used as a kind of workroom and studio where Eva painted.

At first, it was a good situation, because I would look after their kid. He always fell asleep when they went out. I would have the run of the house. They didn't own a TV, but they had a ton of books and magazines. I read and drank a glass of wine. They returned late in the evening and sat down to eat something before going to bed. They became closer during those nights out at the jazz clubs in Seattle or the Blue Moon Tavern in Seattle, where they visited some of Jim's old college buddies and sometimes went to parties near the University of Washington campus.

It was from Jim and Eva that I learned about Roethke, the greatest poet in the Pacific Northwest. Jim had taken a class from him. "Three months and he told me everything I need to know," Jim said more than once. He referred to his teacher by his last name, not Professor Roethke or Theodore Roethke, but just Roethke.

Still drunk, even after the drive back from Seattle, Jim slurred his way through all of Roethke's poem, "The Lost Son". I had to watch him read it. I stood to say goodnight. Jim stopped reading and asked," Where are you going?" I sat down. He kept on:

The shape of a rat?
It's bigger than that.
It's less than a leg.
And more than a nose.
> *Just under the water.*
> *It usually goes.*

"We were at a party with Roethke," Jim said. "He was as drunk as everyone else. He was drunker than everyone else, except for the guy who passed out on the lawn. "

I had applied to the University of Washington. My art teacher and Jim wrote me letters of recommendation. I suppose it would have been possible to enroll in Roethke's class. Maybe Roethke could tell me what to do, because although everyone else seemed intent on it, their instructions weren't giving me a clue.

Jim talked sometimes about the artists Kenneth Callahan, Guy Anderson, and Morris Graves. Eva, in turn talked admiringly about an artist who had lived in Vancouver, Emily Carr. But for these artists, who had grown up in places like Edmonds, although they admired them they also had contempt for their orgins. Jim figured they fooled people into considering them great artists. They were all right, but... Roethke, however, didn't come from anywhere around here. He had ascended from elsewhere, a cloud island drifting over Ireland crowded with a hodgepodge of poets, a veritable anthology of English verse: Dylan Thomas, Keats, T.S. Elliot, and so on. Toward Roethke there wasn't any jealousy, just reverence.

Through January and February that year I thought I was the luckiest girl in school, because I had escaped from my parents' house and I had escaped from the street, and I was living with a writer and his artist wife—this seemed like a perfect combination to me—and I looked after their peaceful one-year-old.

But gradually Eva became suspicious of me. I'm not sure how it started. She began to give me more chores. At first, she liked me to be downstairs watching after the baby while she painted. Jim was upstairs grading papers, and I was downstairs drawing and painting and verifying that their kid didn't kill himself. Eventually, Eva said she needed to do her work in her peace. So I took the baby out in the stroller and visited the river. I tried very carefully to do exactly as she said.

I was accepted to the university that autumn with a scholarship and a grant. That night we had a big dinner in my honor and numerous bottles of wine. Jim became very drunk and suggested that after the baby went to sleep, "Lets all get naked!" Tipsy herself, Eva just giggled. I went to lay the baby down and was wondering what he meant, "Let's all get naked?" When I returned upstairs, Jim and Eva had gone into the bedroom. The door was ajar, and I could hear them. I couldn't tell whether I should go in there as well, and so I sat on the couch. They finally came out. They played Mingus while I picked up the dishes and washed them, and then I sat on the floor and drank a glass of wine. Eva looked at me. "Congratulations, honey," she said.

"Thanks," I said. I was happy again, and I didn't think about the weird incident again until a couple of nights later when I came home and Eva and the baby were gone and it was just Jim and me in the house.

"She finally left us alone," he said.

"Where is she?" I asked.

"She's at her mother's house. Her father isn't doing well and needs help. "

"Shouldn't you be with them?"

"I have papers to grade."

"Shouldn't you be grading them?"

"I graded them already," he said. "After three years of reading these papers, I've already read everything these kids are capable of writing."

"What does that mean?" I asked.

"Personal essays," he said. "Individual expression is

fine, but seventeen year old kids aren't individuals."

"Is that how you felt about me?"

"I'm not talking about you. I'm talking about the students in class where I work."

When he said this, I thought he was giving me a pass. I thought maybe I was no longer just one of those students in the class where he worked.

He got out a bottle of wine, and he put on Mingus. We ate cheese and slices of ham for dinner and oranges for desert. After we finished the bottle of wine, he opened another.

I kissed him because he wanted me to kiss him. I hadn't thought about boys one way or the other the entire year— being more concerned with where I was going to sleep. We were on the couch drinking wine and kissing and pretty soon I was folded up under him, and I had to pee. I wanted him to stop, but then I didn't want to be rude. I had never done this before, and then I started to cry when I realized what had happened and that I still had to pee. I jumped up and went to the bathroom and half expected blood or something, but there wasn't anything I wouldn't expect.

When I came back he was saying, even before I got there, "It's okay. It's okay." We sat on the couch listening to the record. It came to the end. The needle lifted and ratcheted into its slot. "You should make sure to brush your teeth," he said.

When I woke, Eva was back and so was the baby. I could hear the baby crying. I went upstairs, drank cold coffee still in the pot, and dressed for school. School had lost its importance. The kids there were obsessed with baseball

games and now in the spring with the sequence of parties
and dances leading up to graduation it all seemed quaint.
I liked sitting with my old friends, and listening to them
talk, but what they were talking about had nothing to do
with me.

Eva suggested I move out. She found an apartment for
me near the University District. She said I would have to
find a job or something in order to pay the rent, but I had
my own place.

"But what about the help with the baby?"

"We'll figure it out," Eva said. "I don't think it works
having you in the house with Jim and me. You've been a
wonderful guest."

She took me to the apartment, and I couldn't believe I
would have my very own place. Already, Jim had moved a
few pieces of furniture there, old things they didn't need.
He wasn't there. I could tell from Eva's careful expression
that I shouldn't ask about him. Eva said to me, "Good
luck," and shook my hand, and then left me alone. I had a
door I could lock.

I slept there the first night. I woke in the middle of the
night imagining that a sailor was sitting in the corner. I
could hear sounds outside in the street. In the morning,
I dressed and walked down the block and came to a
boulevard filled with used bookstores. A cat languished in
one window. People played music. Kids sat on one of the
walls and smoked, then beyond that there was the campus
where I would go after the summer.

I walked across the campus and thought maybe I
would see Roethke. Maybe he would be there somewhere

teaching people to write poetry? The campus was filled with wild plants, huge rhododendrons, and gigantic trees that I couldn't even see the tops of unless I stopped and stared right up at the sky.

Nothing had happened in my life to make me what I was, and yet I was a person, even if people like Jim and Eva didn't know what to do with me, besides doing what any drunken sailor would do, which was to make me do things for them. They didn't want to hear what I had to say or what I had to think. They liked an audience. I wondered if I could draw or paint or write or do something that anyone would be interested in? I had this image of myself as one of those portrait artists down by the waterfront, painting people who stopped. Everyone was interested in his own portrait.

Walking through the campus with its view of Mount Rainier and the distant choppy water on Lake Washington and the Cascade Mountains I wondered why the school had been built to look the way it did. It looked the way a college campus was supposed to look, and this made me suspicious. There were gothic buildings, lead-paned glass, a general Cambridge-Oxford-Harvard pastiche. It looked real enough, but the overall effect was chintzy and put on. I could pretend to be anywhere. The view was the one thing that wrecked the illusion that this was some real institution of higher learning.

It occurred to me I could see Roethke if he was here. I could find where he was and go to his class. I went to the library and found a map and asked where I could find the English Department. An old woman at the department said

Roethke taught class on Tuesdays and Thursdays at 2:30 in Denny Room 213. I would skip school the next day to see him.

That night, I found a job waiting tables. I read books in my apartment and drew pictures at the Formica table. In the morning, I caught the bus to school, though. I didn't want to return. Jim paid no attention to me during the class. I left school at noon and took the bus back to Seattle and went to stand outside Room 213.

I stood in the hallway and looked at the students arrive one by one. They came in and looked out the window. They leaned on the desks. They smoked and chatted. 2:30 came and went. No one resembling a teacher came. At 2:45 a thickset man, not fat exactly, but fleshy and dripping with sweat, his tie flung over one shoulder, rushed up to the door. He paused to breath in heavily, and then he blanched when he saw the students in the room. He looked at me standing in the hallway. "Do you need help?" he asked me. He kept trying to catch his breath.

"I'm going to be a student here in the autumn," I said.

"You do need help but that is beyond my powers," he said. "I think a handful of reputable universities are still accepting applications. You will need to make haste."

He seemed perfectly happy standing in the hallway. He was a man with freely wandering eyes. He looked at me from head to chest. That seemed to calm him down.

"Are you the teacher?" I asked.

"I'm the professor," he said. He seemed glad that I had asked because he reached for the door. "I don't teach."

He threw open the door. "Class!" he hollered with a

deep-throated burst, and launched into some speech as the door closed. I watched him through the glass in the door where it seemed safer, although the class appeared unmoved by his shout. He glanced back at me to confirm the effectiveness of his entrance. After he turned, I left the musty school building down the marble steps to where I could feel the wind racing over Lake Washington and through the too tall trees. What did he mean, "I don't teach?" Wasn't that the job of a teacher to tell students what to do? Everyone wanted me to do what he said. I realized I didn't know what I wanted to do myself, but I would do something.

Being Dead

With sincerest apologies to *Being Dead* by Jim Crace

E ven the dead have love lives. Simon had a love life, too, although he had never shared the details of it with anyone, well, anyone alive. Partly this was because Simon was shy. The woman at the home said he was *reticent*. She was a nice woman. She was old and often wore slippers throughout the day. Simon often considered that he should buy her new slippers, but he never had the money. He once went to the Marks and Spencer and browsed the slippers. He picked up a pair to purchase. He had the statement ready in his mind and muttered it himself as he considered it. "I'm buying these for my mum. Her slippers are worn out." He repeated the phrase many times in preparation for handing the slippers to the pretty young woman who operated the cash register. She had brown hair in wisps that clung to the air just above her neck. Simon stood near a stack of chocolate gift boxes. The security guard noted him. The man wore clothes similar to anyone else: a black blazer with the sleeves rolled to his elbows and blue jeans with a few holes in them. However, he had a very fine black line that coiled into his ear. Simon always kept a watch for these men because they seemed to know him. He didn't know how they knew him, but they knew someone like him didn't belong in a shop like this.

Simon didn't know his parents. He had been told by one of the women who worked in the house where he did grow up that he had been alive when they were alive. At first, he went to school in the regular school, but then one day they took him and put him with other kids who were like him. He didn't know that he was unlike the regular children, until he was placed with the irregular ones. Among them, he recognized himself. One boy peed his pants nearly every day. One girl talked to her aunt who wasn't there. She talked into the air like some people talk on phones. She said her aunt comforted her. All of the children found the stimulation of the florescent light irritating. The tubes of electrified air pulsed and burned a tiny hole of absolute pain in the very center of Simon's brain. The other children in that room felt that way about it as well. They all discussed their sensitivity at some length. The instructor and his assistant kept the light off during the day. They worked by the light of the windows. After a year, Simon liked that room. What he liked most about that room was that Nigel was in that room, too, and Nigel lived in the home but wouldn't talk to him in the home. He talked to no one inside the school either. At break, Simon and Nigel would run to the far edge of the playground and find frogs, baby birds, ants, any thing living or dead, and examine their sex parts. The little creatures forgotten by the rest of the world belonged to them. They could do as they liked. They did. Nigel liked them to be alive; but once he finished, then Simon could have a go.

They caught a squirrel once. The squirrel was very fascinating, to be sure, because it had fur and seemed almost like a human being compared to a frog or butterfly. A boy from another class discovered them and thought they were playing with the dead animal. "They can have diseases," the boy said and he took the dead squirrel away from Simon. The boy gave Simon a weird look. Simon didn't know whether that was because he realized Simon was from the room with the lights off during the day or if he knew what Simon had been doing to the squirrel. Simon was quite worked up by it. He was more worked up then he would get when he climbed the rope in gym, where he liked to squeeze the thick, hemp rope between his legs and pull his privates along its length. The feeling of the rope running over his privates filled Simon's entire body with a feeling like the meat had been removed from under his skin and filled with marshmallows.

The other boy took the squirrel away from Nigel and Simon. He took it away because at the time the squirrel, like a free animal, didn't belong to itself, it belonged to

Simon. He was the one who had it, and then the boy took the squirrel away and he owned it. Simon let the boy take it because Simon didn't want to talk and let his words enter that boy's head where that boy would have even more thoughts about Simon. Simon didn't want to exist to that boy. He let the boy take the squirrel and was glad when the boy was gone.

Simon's history of sex was short because he realized later, after he had left school and tried to work a trade and then lost a job, that he loved the body parts of human beings but not the being parts of humans. People thought all kinds of bad things in their beings, and usually they said the bad things they were thinking, which also meant they had even worse, secret things that they thought that they did not say. People were always changing. Just looking at one you didn't know what it was thinking, and even if it told you, you didn't know. Not so with a body.

So far the best moment in Simon's life was when he lived in a rooming house in Cardiff. A drug addict downstairs named Eileen overdosed. Simon knew that such a thing was possible, and it had been something he thought about when he saw Eileen. The woman was young, and wore a long cotton dress with sleeves. She looked as if she came from a pen and ink drawing: black hair, dark lips, and mascara around her eyes. She was plump, but grew a little skinnier while Simon knew her. One morning Simon went downstairs, and he peered into her room. There she was, prone on her sofa with the TV still running and Simon knew she was no longer alive. He went into the room and locked the door. He had the best ten minutes of his life.

Shortly thereafter, though, a policewoman came to ask him questions about Eileen. They took from Simon a swab from his mouth. They talked to him and wrote it down. He didn't tell them, but later they knew. They knew she had died, and they knew he had sex with her after she had died and was dead. What did it matter? The policewoman told him that they would note what he did. They were going to keep him under watch.

He learned they knew because he had ejaculated, and his ejaculate contained information like words that the police knew how to read. They could read his name in the ejaculate. At the time, Simon thought once in a lifetime is enough for a lifetime like his. But the memory of the woman, inert, her skin as lustrous as the bottom of a porcelain bowl, grew within him until Simon could no longer think about it or it would fill with him such longing and despair he got goose bumps and wanted to pull his body parts off.

Simon lived in another home. Simon liked the home because it was near a beach where dead crabs and fish washed ashore, and Simon could examine them. This home for grown ups was very bad indeed because some of the people were always paying attention to Simon. Simon liked it when no one paid any attention to him at all. They told Simon things because they knew that no one asked Simon anything. And Simon assumed—to say he realized this is to overstate it—that Simon wouldn't remember what they had told him. To them, Simon was a human-shaped object that could nod its head and express astonishment at the things they told him.

A man returned from the beach. The man wore a new lime-green sweater and carried a paper bag bunched into a flower in his hand. The man had told Simon many things about the crimes he committed. The man did things that no one else would do. He stole a car and drove it into a wall. He got out before it went into the wall. The man often robbed people in other towns. Sometimes he used a knife, and with the knife the people would give him things. This had happened just now. The man said he had robbed a couple that was fucking on the beach. The man shook his head. "It was a sight you would not want to see, old Simon." The man then told Simon that they resisted the robbery, and he had to do what had to be done. He used a rock instead of a knife.

"Are they still there?"

The man was startled that Simon asked. Simon had never made any comments on the man's narratives about robberies and arson. The man shook his head. "The tide has come in. The police have come around."

Simon nodded and stared at the sky. The man lost interest in Simon, and then Simon went to the beach. He hurried. If the tide was going to come in, they would get washed to sea and ruined.

He thought about them. A man and a woman. In his thought he imagined a couple like Eileen and a boy who looked just like her, long black hair, thin arms and legs, plump stomach, and pale skin resting peacefully on a beach blanket with their hands folded.

He came to the beach and late in the day; he discovered a slightly damp magazine resting at a strange angle on a bush in the dunes. *The Entomology*, it said; although to Simon it was just a glossy object with the letter shapes. He could read, but just barely, and so for him words retained their magical properties, their boundaries of letter shapes. And then in a protected dell, with a thick patch of grass and protected from the wind and easy view, Simon discovered the remains of Joseph and Celice. Cecile was a large woman sprawled near a beach blanket much like the one Simon had imagined. Her head was a mass of bloody hair. Her face was still intact, mostly, and she seemed to be completely at rest. Her skirt had been removed and lay neatly folded on the blanket still. She stared into the sky as if waiting for a headache to pass. The man, however, smelled like a shadowy corner of a street where the bums pee. He was nude, not thin exactly. Skin draped from his arms and chest, his buttocks, and a matte of gray hair lay tangled on his chest. Streaks of blood and some other substance ran from the wounds in his head. One bloody hand was lifted, as if he was pointing, but he didn't point anywhere.

Simon was startled. His breath came out in puffs from combing the beach and his anticipation, and now he discovered not what he expected but instead the scene of a crime. Flies, not swarming exactly, but industriously worked on the man. Another sortie had set up shop in profusion in the wounds under the woman's hair.

Simon would have to find the police.

He turned to leave and then stood at the top of the dune. There was no one for as far as he could see. Dusk was coming. Soon it would be dark. How would he talk to them? The thought of saying anything to the police filled him with a cool, dreadful burn. He thought of the woman, her patch of pubic hair, her long, orange colored legs, and the yellow calluses on her heels. He could lift her leg and move it, and nothing would happen.

He turned back. He grabbed the blanket and shook it out and tossed it over the man.

He grabbed the woman and pulled her across the grass. He used a stray bag to shoo the flies away. Three tiny crabs scurried from under her. They had black shells. Simon dragged the woman to a place with a thick matte of grass. He held his nose while he brushed the back of her legs. Her skin was cool to the touch and was faintly gray and translucent, the surface of it the color of the edge of an ice cube. There weren't any other crabs or insects near her now. He pulled her shirt over her head. Her breasts were in her bra. He pulled a breast from a cup. She had a tiny areola and a tidy nipple. He pinched it. After the first time, Simon had bought a condom from a bathroom. He kept it in his wallet in the way that he had heard about. He removed it from his wallet, and then after three minutes with Cecile, he deposited his ejaculate into it. He then carefully removed it. He felt peace from the nagging sensation that he had been drowning in for the years since Eileen. He pulled this woman's shirt back over her head, and then dragged her back to her old spot. He threw the beach blanket back. He still held the small latex bag filled with fluid. He tucked it back within the condom wrapper and then put it inside the stray bag. He left, walking now through the darkness and under the faint light from the cloudy sky. The dunes were just shadows. They were above the tide now.

The phrase from Willy Wonka kept going through Simon's head, "A lifetime supply of chocolate." Simon disposed of the bag in a public restroom garbage, washed his hands, and then went to find some fish and chips. In the dunes, in the darkness, more crabs, and beetles, and in the morning sea gulls set to work.